Ironheart

IRONHEART

J. Boyett

SALTIMBANQUE BOOKS

NEW YORK

For Mary Sheridan.

For Pam Carter, Dawn Drinkwater, and Andy Shanks.

Acknowledgments

Many thanks to Kelly Kay Griffith for having read the manuscript and given valuable advice.

And thanks to you for reading! Please consider visiting me at www.jboyett.net and signing up for my mailing list.

Ironheart

One

The *Canary* formed itself a patch at a time, unmelting back from the void as it came out of hyperspace. If anyone had been watching, even most computers, it would have seemed to pop into existence instantaneously. But in fact it did reappear piece by piece, the sequence of those appearances being arranged by a system so complex as to look random to almost any known intelligence.

The fat gray bulb of the ship floated in space a moment before heading toward Planet XB-79853-D7-4. The hyperdrive that made up most of the ship's bulk existed only in hyperspace and was undetectable in this dimension—ninety-nine percent of what showed up in realspace was the vast curve of the cargo hold; there was a box attached to that curve that was given over to living quarters, far away from that box were the thrusters, and here and there on the smooth surface were sprays of antennae. The ship's realspace thrusters were modest, but it would reach its destination soon enough. The pilot, Willa, was a highly skilled intuiter and had managed to bring them back to reality deep within the solar system itself.

As usual, once they were back in realspace, Willa collapsed into sobs, slumping over so dramatically it seemed she would slide right out of the pilot's chair. The transparent half-sphere of the intuition bowl remained suspended over her head.

There were three men in the pilot's room with her, the rest of the crew. Fehd, the captain and owner of the *Canary*, was grinning lopsidedly; it was the nervous grimace he always wore when Willa cried. He pulled a medallion out from under his shirt and kissed it, then tucked it back under his clothes. It was a way of thanking some goddess local to his homeworld for safe passage. He pushed his blue cap further back on his head and managed to keep grinning while still looking like he wished he were somewhere else. Madaku, who was primarily the engineer, gazed down at Willa with tender concern, wishing as always that he could make this transition easier for her.

Burran, the security specialist, Willa's lover, paid no attention to her fit. Madaku always thought Burran should try to console her—in Madaku's opinion he was too crude and insensitive for Willa. In any case, it was clear that the man had trouble looking at her when she came out of the intuition bowl. Burran moved to the nearest console and checked the readings.

"Everything checks out," he muttered. "She brought us in adequately far from any danger points, but right in close to the target planet. Amazing control."

A renewed flurry of tears burst out of her. Burran ignored it.

Madaku slipped over to join Burran at the console. Making as if he were also there to study the readings, he instead murmured, "Maybe you should be more interested in comforting her, when she brings us out of hyperspace."

Burran narrowed his eyes at Madaku in a disdainful smirk, as if to say that Madaku wanting to sleep with Willa didn't give him the right to tell Burran what to do. Madaku felt a blush blazing over his pale skin.

"Excessive worry can be an insult, you know," said Burran. Unlike Madaku, he didn't bother to keep his voice low—Willa wouldn't be able to understand them yet. "You don't need to be so concerned over Willa. Do you know what her scores were, at the intuiters' academy? This ship is damn lucky to have her—she's going to wind up being one of the greatest pilots of all time. She was trained in the Jeatty hyperfield method, you know."

Madaku found it shocking that the guy could be so cavalier about his lover's suffering. As for her having been trained in the Jeatty method, that was one of the reasons they'd gotten her cheap. Pilots had been intuiting their way through the hyperfield just fine for thousands of years, and non-humans had been doing it for millennia before that—after all this time and experience, there was almost a whiff of madness around a belated innovator like Jeatty.

Embarrassed, still grinning, pushing his cap back and forth on his head, Fehd came over, to discreetly break them up and also to get some distance from Willa. "So what we got?"

Madaku was too flustered to answer, so it was a good thing Fehd was talking to Burran. Switching his attention away from Madaku and back to the console, the beefy brown-skinned security specialist squinted his blue eyes at the readings. "Looks good," he said. "So far everything matches what the surveys decided centuries ago. Planet has a little more than two G's mass. Thick atmosphere, poisonous to us. Could be some pretty rocks for us to take home. But like we figured, the easy money's in the orbiting planetoids. Great big cloud of everything from pebbles to moonlets, millions of them."

No surprises. The only thing remotely exotic about XB-79853-D7-4 was its location—the system's star was one of the very last sparks before the great intergalactic dark. Most of the "stars" visible off the *Canary*'s bow were in fact galaxies.

But not even that was particularly interesting. After all, there were many millions of other stars, also out on the edge of the galactic rim.

Madaku double-checked Burran's findings. He nodded. "There'll be more than enough minerals to make the trip profitable."

Fehd rubbed his palms. "Nice," he said. "Not like Lohani." The *Canary* did the mildly dangerous (or, really, just mildly unpredictable) work of exploring systems that had been catalogued centuries ago, or millennia, but never yet actually visited by sentients. In return they got first pickings of the mineral resources. The scopes were accurate enough that almost nobody ever got stuck visiting a system that lacked adequate resources to make the trip worthwhile—anyone who checked knew what they'd find beforehand. But one time, seven years ago, Fehd had somehow wound up at a system called Lohani

5

that turned out to be nothing but dirt and ice and common rocks, and the unprofitable trip haunted him. Neither Madaku nor Burran had been with him then. Willa hadn't been with him either, of course—she'd joined up when Burran had.

They brought the ship into orbit while Willa calmed down, gradually coming back out of the state of wobbly vulnerability the hyperspace-interface (the hyperface) put her into: that fluctuating mental state in which the layers of personality and socialization between her deep-rooted computational abilities and the symbol logic governing her real-world choose-reflexes all melted away. Often she came out of the hyperface with a psychedelic uncertainty as to her name, gender, language, age, and general place in the roil of history, unable to decide whether her personal memories or her memories of various vids, novels, and rumors were the better, truer representation of whatever the "self" was she was meant to be looking for. It wasn't so extreme as that, this time—but always, she spilled out of the intuition bowl in a thick soup of anger, grief, glee, horniness, confusion, and fear.

But soon enough she was able to join the three men on the observation deck, a pink blanket wrapped around her shoulders and a steaming mug of tea between her palms, face red from crying and from scrubbing the tears and snot away. She laughed at herself easygoingly. It seemed to Madaku that Willa was trying to comfort Burran, to signal to him through gestures, glances, and intonations that everything was all right. It was almost as if she were the one making apologies, for having upset him by getting upset herself. Even though it didn't seem to bother her, it offended Madaku that she should be the one to have to make that effort. It wouldn't have been that way if she had been with Madaku instead. There was nothing special about Burran, nothing he gave Willa that Madaku couldn't.

Though he hated to admit to such petty jealousy, Madaku couldn't hide it from himself, at least. Why *shouldn't* Willa have been with him? He was just as special as anyone else was.

The cloudy green-blue swirl of XB-79853-D7-4 filled three-quarters of the observation window, bright and beautiful

6

in the gleaming white frame of the deck's walls. Fehd whipped up a bunch of pink hula-berry doughnuts from the protein matrix and brought them to the others on a tray. It was customary for the intuiter to name a planet that had been physically contacted for the first time, but none of the *Canary*'s crew got too excited over the honor. For one thing, even if no known intelligence had ever visited this system, it had been catalogued millennia ago by simple telescopes, along with the couple hundred billion other planets in the galaxy, and its properties had long since been analyzed more fully by remote spectroscopy. When the Galactic Registry had first been set up, over seven thousand years ago, XB-79853-D7-4 had been uploaded. In the intervening time it had caught the interest of half a dozen scientists and prospective miners, three of whom had dubbed it with their own sobriquets, one in a human language that the modern humans of the *Canary* could no longer recognize, and two in alien tongues, whose sounds they didn't even try to parse.

So it was kind of a silly custom. Still, whatever name Willa chose would go into the Galactic Registry, where it would stand alongside the catalogue-name of XB-78953-D7-4 as the planet's official word-name. It would probably continue to be used, especially if the *Canary* managed to set up a profitable exploitation-chain. So it was not a name that would be forgotten, at least.

Sipping her tea, gazing experimentally and mischievously up at Burran with her huge eyes, she said, "Maybe I could name the planet Burran?"

Madaku didn't know whether Willa was joking, but Burran seemed to think not: "*No*," he said.

Burran picked up a stray tablet from the tabletop, called up readings, and began grimly scrolling through them. It struck Madaku that the hyperspace trips affected Burran almost as much as they did Willa, but inversely: he clammed up and became even more his sullen, silent, macho self.

Burran continued to scroll through the readings. He said, "You know, XB-79853-D7-4 may be deadly to us, but it's almost a perfect habitat for zyblots." He said this almost with satisfaction, albeit a mirthless one; as if all of a sudden the thing most important to him was depriving Willa of the right to name the planet by proving there might be someone else there first, just to make sure it didn't wind up being called Burran after all.

Of course, Madaku knew that would be a crazy thing for Burran to want, and that he, Madaku, was himself probably just being the asshole.

Fehd stood up and started pushing his cap back and forth again as he walked over to Burran, looking worriedly back over his shoulder at the planet in the window. "But there's no evidence of zyblots, is there?" The eccentric zyblots had been known to set up colonies in remote areas and go centuries without registering them. But even an unregistered settlement would still control the exploitation rights for the planet and its orbiting planetoids.

Except, Madaku reminded himself, there was no reason to suspect a zyblot settlement was here, other than the bare possibility of it. Either Burran was having fun stirring up shit, or else this was his paranoid security training.

Fehd was obsessively confirming and reconfirming that they hadn't actually seen a settlement. Burran kept calmly shaking his head, acting like he'd never implied that they had. Since Fehd kept asking, Burran shrugged and told him he would amp up the sensor power to begin a more thorough sweep of the planet and its environs.

Fehd grimaced and winced, probably regretting his big mouth. Madaku was annoyed. On the off-chance that there *was* a settlement below, one not actively broadcasting its presence, their ideal scenario would be to not notice it. Then they would have zero legal obligations. Actively *looking* for someone was crazy.

Burran might say that it was always a good idea to do a sweep, in case the hypothetical undetected presence was a threat. But, while there were still some irrationally belligerent space-faring species out there, most of their members had been wiped out during one of the Great Galactic Hygienes. It was true that the occasional individual psychopath did get hold of a ship; still, it was absurd to go looking for enemies. In a galaxy where resources could be plucked from any one of billions of worlds no one had yet had time to visit, where the worst annoyance you had to worry about was that you'd find a system occupied and so would have to move on to the next one, why should anyone fight?

Burran kept his eyes on the tablet and the planet outside the window throughout his discussion with Fehd. He spoke with a nonchalant professionalism and acted like he didn't notice his other two crewmates. But something about the amused, possibly sad way Willa kept eyeing him suggested to Madaku that she also believed he really had gone off on this tangent at least partly because he'd been embarrassed by the suggestion that the planet be named after him.

Eventually Fehd and Burran left for the bridge. All the same data was available from each console or tablet in every room of the ship—the only advantage of the bridge was that there were bigger walls to project the readouts upon, and being more easily able to enlarge or shrink or otherwise move around the images aided in thinking problems through. By rights, Madaku should have accompanied them while they all left Willa to finish recovering. Neither man beckoned to him, though. Madaku thought there was pointed, deliberate contempt in the way Burran declined to look his way. As if he were saying, *See how little it threatens me for you to be alone with my woman.*

Madaku watched Willa a few moments. Her gaze stayed on the beautiful silent planet filling the window. Madaku waited for her dreamy eyes to flicker up his way, but they remained fixed upon the world she'd guided them to. Eventually he said, "He should have just gone ahead and let you name the planet. That's your right, after all."

She looked up at him, startled. Madaku acknowledged that it was weird, the way he was almost trying to comfort Willa for not having been able to name a world after the man he considered his rival. There was no trace of hard feelings in

9

Willa's bright voice as she said, "Oh, no—I just teased him a little too hard, is all. And anyway, he's right, we *should* do a thorough sweep. That's the only way to be safe, technically."

Madaku's mouth twisted as if he had something sour in it. He nearly said something critical about the paranoid level of Burran's zeal. Instead, he said, "I don't think he has any right to be difficult, right when you come out of the hyperface. That's when you should be, you should be pampered."

Willa didn't turn her head, but her eyes slid his way. Madaku withered under that gentle look, and tried to tell himself he was misinterpreting it: a mild mixture of amusement, apprehension, pity, and offense.... As for the apprehension, who could blame her for that? Surely, on such a tiny ship, for him to threaten the group's stability by coming between the security specialist and the intuiter must be irresponsible. He should be working harder to control himself.

He couldn't help it, was all. When Burran and Willa had joined the *Canary* a year ago, Madaku had had no personal feelings about either of them, aside from a mild distaste for Burran. Gradually, though, he'd become all but obsessed with Willa. He couldn't even have said why—it was just that he had a sense that she was something special, that there wasn't anyone else quite like her. Of course that was ridiculous. There were trillions of other humans in the galaxy, not to mention all the other sentients. Any one individual's traits must be reproduced a billion times over.

He lowered his gaze, dreading that she might call attention to his indiscretion.

Instead, she gave him a bright smile, and said, "He only gets that way because he can't stand it, seeing me suffer when there's nothing he can do."

Two

It turned out that someone *had* beaten them to XB-79853-D7-4. When Burran delivered them the news, in his deadpan way, Fehd clapped his hands over his face and swore an oath by one of his goddesses. Madaku threw up his arms in disgust. Willa gazed worshipfully at Burran as if he were the most ingenious sleuth the ages had ever known: "How did you ever *find* them?"

Burran shrugged. "Looked," he said.

They could discuss the situation in any room in the ship, but for the sake of formality Burran called them to the Discussion Room. The small white room's walls were covered with detachable tablets functioning as monitors, but that was true of most of the ship. The Discussion Room's distinguishing feature was the round white table in its center. They all entered the room together, grabbed a tablet off the wall, and took the first seat which presented itself.

The good news, said Burran, was that it wasn't a settlement. At least, he'd so far found no evidence of one—only a lone ship. A ship by itself would have no exploitation rights, unless and until it registered a claim with the Galactic Registry.

"Well, then, our first step should be to register that claim ourselves," said Fehd.

"I already did that." One could hear in Burran's voice that he considered it obvious that he would have done so. "There was no conflicting claim."

Fehd spoke with cautious relief: "So, as long as we don't find a settlement?..."

11

"This ship by itself would have no basis for a claim," confirmed Burran.

"Wonderful!" Fehd turned from Burran back to Madaku, seated across from him. "In that case, we better get the extraction process prepped." And he launched into a discussion of their equipment and how it should be dispersed among the planet's cloud of orbiting planetoids.

But Burran interrupted them: "Wait!" Fehd and Madaku stared at Burran in surprise. He glared back at them in disbelief, and said, "Before we start dispersing the equipment and getting preoccupied with the mineral sifts, we need to head around the planet and take a closer look at this ship."

Ah. It was a security thing. Madaku thought the life of a security specialist must be a frustrating one: all those years of training, and then most of them never encountered a dangerous situation in their whole lives. And if anyone did attack them the *Canary*'s AI would take defensive and evasive action a lot faster than any of its human complement could. The only one among them who truly had to face danger was Willa, when she put on the intuition bowl and hooked herself up to the hyperface: not physical danger, but the terrifying prospect of never finding her way back to her conscious mind, of ending as a drooling meat-sack whose identity was forever misplaced. Not for the first time, Madaku speculated that this risk imbalance was probably a cause for stress in her relationship with Burran.

And yet she grinned at the three men and said, "I don't guess I could just hyperjump us over to the other ship?"

Fehd smiled tightly, a surely-you-jest smile. "It's only a ten-minute ride," he said. "It seems like an extremely dangerous risk just to shave off a few minutes."

"I was only kidding, of course," she replied, as if Fehd were being silly. Then she couldn't help adding, "Though I bet I *could* do it."

Madaku stared at her. He believed she was serious—he believed that if Fehd in some fit of insanity had given his consent, she would have gone through with it. Why anyone would want

12

to court the miserable wild distress that intuiters were plunged into, Madaku couldn't imagine; not to mention that it would be inconceivably dangerous, performing such a tight jump whose start-point and end-point would be in such close proximity to each other, as well as to so many massive bodies.

For the first time since Willa had come out of the bowl, Burran was smiling. It was a difficult smile to read, though. Studying his lover, he said, "She really could, you know. She's the best intuiter in the galaxy."

The notion that the *Canary* had just happened to wind up with the best intuiter in the galaxy was a bit too rich to swallow, thought Madaku; but whatever, the hyperbole of a lover, and all that.

He still didn't think Burran was good enough for her, but he had to admit they made an interesting couple: with Burran being one of the only people he'd ever met who viscerally *believed* in danger, and Willa the only one who courted it, even in jest.

Fehd got them back on track. Almost as if he were humoring Burran, he said, "You think this ship could be a threat, Burran?"

"Anything *could* be a threat. If there's a crew aboard, and it's not connected to a settlement, and it's not here to prospect, then why *is* it here? For all we know, they could be bandits, hiding out."

Even Willa had trouble not making a face at that one. Space-bandits were exceedingly rare, and none of them had ever encountered any, nor met anyone who had. However, they did occasionally exist. With a bare hint of mockery, Fehd said, "You think they may be bandits? In that case, maybe we ought to give them a wide berth."

Burran tensed his mouth. "Except that, if there are intelligences on board that ship, they probably already know we've seen them. If they don't want to be found, that could create problems for us. Anyway, I didn't say they were bandits, I only pointed out that's one possibility among many. More likely, the ship is a derelict. I'm not picking up much from inside—it has your basic scramblers installed. But, to judge by the radiation traces along its thrusters, I'd say it's been here a long time."

Fehd rubbed his smooth chin thoughtfully. "Of course, they could be in suspended animation...."

"It may have been there a *long* time," Burran repeated. "If the readings are correct, the ship's been there derelict long enough that it would be pushing the limit of any suspended-animation technology that the Registry has on file. And it may have already pushed far past it."

"If the crew's dead, the ship's scrap." Now Fehd sounded excited. "Is the boat interesting?"

"I haven't been able to find a match for it in the Galactic Registry," said Burran.

There was a moment's stillness from the other three. Now, *that* was unusual.

Not unheard-of, though. Madaku recovered and said, "So it's probably a custom job. And if it really never was registered, I guess that would lend credence to Burran's theory that there's something nefarious about it."

"That's not my theory," Burran testily corrected. "I just pointed out it's a possibility."

Madaku pretended Burran hadn't said anything. "I'm interested in seeing the specs from the unknown ship. I'll call them up after we're done here. Go ahead and send me any special observations you've made, as well."

The three men were nodding at each other, hinting with their body language that they were all ready to adjourn, when Willa said, "Hey, but wait a minute."

Madaku realized guiltily that without noticing he had preemptively dismissed anything she might have to say, which was the kind of thing he was always silently accusing Burran of doing. "Yes, Willa?" he said. "What do you think?"

She was giving all three of them a funny look. "Let's not forget that they're not necessarily a threat, or salvage. They could also still be alive and be stuck out here. Right? There could be people aboard, in trouble. Especially if they're at the upper limit of suspended animation's effectiveness."

The guys all shifted uncomfortably in their seats. Willa looked at them all quizzically. Plainly, it never would have occurred to her to put salvage opportunities ahead of the lives of others; the idea must be completely foreign to her, if she was having so much trouble realizing that was what the guys had done.

"You're right," Burran was saying. "Don't worry, babe—we're going to go over there and check it out."

Maybe she really was a superior creature, Madaku thought, with a kind of schoolboyish yearning. But he knew that was nonsense. It came down to circumstances. All the *Canary's* crewmembers hailed from patriarchal cultures, in which men were generally trained to be harsh and competitive, while women were encouraged to cultivate empathy and tenderness. Such conditioning made it easy for women like Willa to impress men like Madaku, Burran, and Fehd with their angelic natures.

Madaku knew that was all there was to it and it was nothing special. Yet he still got all gooey-eyed around her, anyway.

They cruised to the other side of the planet to check out the ship. The AI had been instructed to prioritize the energy shield and to keep the evasive programs ready, almost as a formality. Also as a formality, they double-checked that their own scramblers were functioning, to discourage anyone aboard the other ship from looking through them and seeing the *Canary's* interior. Of course, anyone rude enough should be able to bypass them. Since the *Canary* crew were planning to board in a rescue/salvage mission, this constituted one of the few occasions on which it was acceptable for their AI to try to break through the other ship's code scramblers. It had already done so, to do a sweep and insure that there were no biologicals aboard in immediate danger. But even if their AI had managed to garner significant data, almost everything it would have learned via that hack would have been compartmentalized in a part of its memory banks that would be very difficult for the *Canary* crew to access, as per the Registry's civility guidelines.

The crew would be told only about dangers to themselves, or about biologicals in danger aboard the derelict.

Any other precautions would have seemed superfluous, and they brought the *Canary* right in close.

"They do have scramblers engaged," said Madaku, his eyes on the tablet he held rather than the natural view of the ship in the sunlight out the window. "But according to our AI it's moot, since the data leaking from their AI is so fragmented and distorted that the interior of the ship is basically opaque."

"It takes a long time for AI's to decay like that," said Fehd. "And computers live a lot longer than people anyway."

Willa stared at the other ship, with an intense expression that was almost a frown.

Well might she frown. They had no way to look into the hyperspace dimension and study the ship's hyperdrive. But its realspace specs were formidable. At the center of the ship was a very large box-shaped compartment, which presumably contained the cargo bays, living quarters and any other personal areas. Fanning out from that, in a shiny X, were four massive realspace thrusters. And attached to the thrusters, apparently wired through them to amp up their firepower, were what looked like energy weapons.

"Are those blasters as strong as it looks like they'd be?" asked Fehd.

"Hard to tell," said Burran. Watching his still, attentive expression, Madaku couldn't tell if the big energy weapons made Burran feel apprehensive, or envious, or what. "Doesn't look like they were fooling around, though."

Burran studied the readouts another few seconds, then said, "Madaku, what the hell is that hull made of?" He highlighted the bizarre readings so that they were emphasized on Madaku's tablet, as well. "You ever seen this stuff before?"

Madaku had already noticed. "No," he said, staring at the read-out. The thrusters and thruster-wings, which seemed not to originally have been part of the same design as the main core, were made of fine but not particularly exotic material. But the

16

main body of the ship, under the encrustation of antennae and other add-ons, was a different story. "It looks indestructible. And the sensors can't pierce it, to see what's inside." He uploaded the specs, and felt the bottom drop out of his belly. "This alloy is not in the Registry!"

Fehd breathed out slowly. Burran said, "Gods damn, this is one exotic ship."

"You see the stump of debris there?" said Madaku. "I think that's where the subspace antenna used to be mounted. Maybe it got knocked off by one of these asteroids; maybe it happened in some sort of accident shortly after they arrived. If they lost their hyperdrive and their subspace antenna, they would have been stranded out here, unable to call for help."

They stared for a silent moment at the vessel. It rotated slowly on its axis as it drifted in orbit. For a moment, they saw the top plane of the thruster-wings flat-on and illuminated by the sun. Hundreds of inscriptions were stamped in black all the way down the wing, all in different scripts. There were even a couple of scripts Madaku recognized as non-human, which was noteworthy since so few intelligences besides humans and their AI's used anything that could properly be called writing.

"Anybody able to read any of that?" asked Fehd.

They watched the thruster wing as it drifted around. Just before the writing was gone from view, Burran said, "There— that one's in Krigian, I can read that. It means something like, 'heart made of iron.' 'Ironheart,' I guess."

They waited. The next thruster wing rose silently into view, flat-on and facing the sun. It, too, was stamped with black-on-white inscriptions, in different writing systems.

They studied it. Willa pointed: "That's in Perse, my grandmother spoke that. I think it says 'Ironheart' too, but it's hard to tell—it's weird. Maybe it's Old Perse."

"And there it is in Pung-tao," Fehd noted. "'Ironheart.'"

And as the third wing rose they could all see it again, this time emblazoned in Old Galactic, just one more inscription among hundreds or thousands: "Ironheart."

"Hand me a tablet," said Fehd. He took it without bothering to notice who'd given it to him and began calling up ships named *Ironheart*. Hundreds of thousands had been uploaded to the Galactic Registry over the millennia, but so far none was turning up that matched this one's specifications.

"*Ironheart*," said Burran, feeling the word in his mouth. "That's a good name for a boat."

Willa didn't take her eyes off the strange new ship; her only response was an expression of distaste.

"How's it look inside, Madaku? Any luck garnering some knowledge from the distorted data leaks?" asked Fehd. They might not be able to look through the hull, but they should be able to pick up enough stray data leakage from the ship's AI to access the ship's own knowledge about its contents. Even with the data corruption, the *Canary* AI ought to be able to glean something useful; and once it had satisfied itself that *Ironheart* was salvage and ergo the *Canary*'s property, it would share that knowledge with the crew.

"Like I told you, our AI claims that what it can see is distorted. But it looks like vacuum inside."

"A dead ship," said Fehd, almost to himself; then, looking at his tablet again, he said, "So all these inscriptions are collated, and they do all say 'Ironheart,' except for a couple languages that aren't in the Registry."

"Aren't in the *Registry*?" repeated Madaku. "Well, they must be made-up, then."

"Probably," said Fehd. "More interesting for us is the fact that all the inscriptions use forms that were current well over a couple thousand years ago. Or more. Like, there's Old Galactic, but no Standard Galactic. Between that and the interior vacuum and the radiation-cold thrusters, I'd say this is a mighty old boat, guys."

"Probably not a lot of tech salvage, then," said Madaku. "But don't underestimate the profit to be gained from historical curiosities, especially in the markets of more primitive societies."

"Sure, sure. I'm not worried about finding a buyer. Right

now, to be honest, I'm more interested in going over and exploring just for the fun of it. Burran, any special concerns, weapons-wise?"

"Nah. Just by the book, is all. Bring along an explosive-based firearm and a knife, in case there's a camouflaged enemy aboard with a hostile AI ready to sabotage our defenses."

Madaku nearly rolled his eyes and almost made a joke about how it would be hard to find the never-used firearms, under the layers of dust. But then that third wing floated up into view again, and he felt a strange, unaccountable chill as again his eyes picked out those words, in Old Galactic: *Ironheart*.

Three

Madaku grabbed a doctor as they left for the little shuttle. There was one or two in every room of the ship—anyone could have grabbed it, but since it was a machine it fell more or less under his purview. The all-purpose, multi-species diagnostic and treatment tool weighed less than a kilo. He mag-clamped the gray metal rectangle to the thigh of his suit; it caused no encumbrance or noticeable weight, and once it was attached he stopped noticing it.

The three men took the little shuttle over to *Ironheart*, while Willa stayed aboard the *Canary*. Madaku, Burran and Fehd were all from worlds with strong patriarchal traditions, so there was an aspect of leaving the damsel behind while they went forth into possible, theoretical danger. Mainly, though, it was standard procedure to leave the intuiter behind when an away team went out. That way, if something happened, the pilot could have the ship primed to go by the time the team returned. Once every ten thousand times or so, something did happen that the hardware and AI's couldn't handle on their own.

Ironheart was a formidable name—Madaku didn't recall having ever heard of a ship called that. As for the *Canary*, that was a traditional name for mining ships. Madaku didn't really know how the custom had begun. He thought a "canary" was a type of bird, and he knew that back in prehistory mining had probably been a dangerous and gloomy affair, in which humans had to break through layers of rock largely via muscle power and then spend large amounts of time in the subterranean dark. He thought of birds as pretty things, and imagined that naming a mining ship *Canary* had originally been a way to celebrate the bright and joyous ease that technology had brought to the mining process; but he really didn't know. Undoubtedly the history of the name was all right there in the Registry. He'd always meant to look it up, but had just never bothered.

The shuttle darted through the vast silence. The three men watched *Ironheart* loom larger and larger till it filled the viewport.

"Look how beat-up it is," said Fehd. "All that pitting and scarring."

"An old ship," murmured Burran. "Madaku, how much of that damage was inflicted here in the system?"

Madaku was already scanning to see whether the molecular traces left by the space rocks that had beaten the ship's hull matched those of XB-79853-D7-4's cloud of moons. "It looks like a lot of them do match," he said. "Between those matches, and the cold radiation trace, I think it's safe to say it's been here a long, long time."

They were already suited up in preparation for the vacuum they expected to find inside the derelict, but they hadn't yet popped their visors closed. Fehd bounced on the balls of his feet, excited about his scavenge. "Hopefully the bodies won't be too gruesome," he said.

The shuttle's autopilot found *Ironheart*'s airlock and pulled them up to it. The men waited to see whether the derelict's circuitry was totally dead, in which case they would force the airlock open, or whether their presence would wake up an AI. (The AI that had been running for untold centuries might be decayed or insane, its mutative function having run out of control during all that time—the mutative function generally led to useful innovation only if it was periodically shepherded, instead of being left to run rampant. But there should be subprograms that had been lying dormant all this while and that would reboot upon being informed of the *Canary* crew's arrival.)

The *Ironheart*'s AI subprograms came to. The shuttle's AI requested access, but *Ironheart* didn't want to give it. So the three men settled in to wait out the computers' fight.

But after thirty seconds Burran and Fehd raised their eyebrows at Madaku, who was following the progress of the hack on his tablet. "Must be some pretty weird code they've got," said Burran.

"I don't care how weird it is," said Madaku. By itself the *Canary*'s AI might have been no match for *Ironheart*'s, but the hyperdrive link in Madaku's tablet connected back to the Registry and gave them its encyclopedic knowledge of all computer language and code ever uploaded, from which they should be able to extrapolate all codes in existence. "There must be examples in the Registry of something at least analogous enough for the AI to figure it out."

"Especially if it's so old," put in Fehd.

"So why aren't the doors opening?" said Burran.

Madaku shook his head in wonder at the readouts. "Looks like this code was rewriting itself and mutating in isolation for a long time before it went to sleep." Then, as if he were arguing with himself, or scolding himself for his own gullibility, he said, "I don't care how long it's been mutating, whatever it was originally extrapolated from must still be in the Registry. Our AI should have found the source code just from this one's deep architecture, and should have back-engineered by now."

Burran gave the other two a significant look. "Maybe it's been mutating in isolation a long, *long* time."

Fehd and Madaku fell silent, vaguely unsettled.

But all computers ultimately ran on math, and no matter how exotic the notation and cognition patterns at the base of this program's architecture, the brute-force computing power of the Registry was ultimately invulnerable. But even once the deep logic architecture had been deciphered, the door didn't open. Madaku said, "Its mutative rate is off the charts. Now our AI's problem is just keeping up. Its workarounds cease to be applicable less than a nanosecond after they're devised."

It wound up taking more than another full minute before the *Ironheart* airlock clanked open. As they made their way through the passage tube over, Fehd said, "We'll get a good amount of credits just for uploading that exotic code into the Registry."

Madaku was too disconcerted to reply. He didn't think the other two men appreciated the magnitude of this code's exoticism—there was no record in the Registry of code with such a fast mutative rate. It had been luck that had allowed the *Canary*'s AI to come up with a workaround that it was able to apply in the nanosecond before the *Ironheart* code shifted enough to make the workaround obsolete. Madaku wasn't confident he would *ever* be able to program translation software that would allow him to establish stable communication with *Ironheart*'s systems, software that mutated at the same rate and in tandem with the other ship's AI.

There was no artificial gravity in the derelict. That was no surprise. But, as they were shining the flashlight through the gloomy crypt of the docking bay, Fehd exclaimed, "Hey, we're pressurizing!"

The other two could already see that, in the readouts displayed on the insides of their visors.

"Pumps still work," marveled Madaku.

Burran said, "Whoever they were, maybe they abandoned ship and hoped to come back someday, since they didn't take their surplus atmosphere."

"Or maybe something killed them all of a sudden and their atmosphere leaked out over eons," said Madaku.

Burran nodded. "Though there doesn't seem to be a leak, so far. I guess we'll find out."

"This is human-breathable air, right?" asked Fehd, an exploratory hand floating up toward his helmet toggle.

"For crying out loud, don't take your fucking helmet off," said Burran. "You know good and well it's impossible for the scanners to check for every single thing in the galaxy that could possibly kill you."

Every once in a while Fehd got pissy, when he felt his dignity as ship's captain was being impugned. "You can never be sure of *everything*," he snapped, floating upside-down relative to his comrades.

"No, but you can at least wait till we've checked with more than these rinky-dink prelims."

Madaku stayed out of it. He knew where Fehd was coming from—"rinky-dink" was hardly a fair description of modern preliminary scans, and he shared the captain's urge to remove the helmet. The odds were a million-to-one against the sensors missing something deadly to humans. But, technically, Burran was right that they should guard against the millionth chance.

Another reason Madaku stayed out of it was that the ship was more interesting than the bickering. As he was panning across with his flashlight, the lights began to flicker on, and soon the place was adequately though dimly illuminated. *Ironheart*, it seemed, had a fairly vigorous welcome-home program, and it made Madaku a little nervous to see the ship's computer doing so much before the *Canary*'s AI had entirely learned to communicate with it. Given the apparent decay of the AI when seen from without, he was taken aback that everything aboard seemed to be working so well.

They were in a large room, across from an open doorway leading out into a corridor. Dust motes were swirling in the still-flickering, bluish fluorescents now that the atmosphere had returned. This room contained many plastic and metal crates, of various sizes. They were stacked in racks that held them immobile in the zero-G. Although the stacks were neat, the crates' varieties of sizes and materials gave the room a jumbled, cluttered feel. All the crates had code scramblers engaged, and since the *Canary*'s crewmen were civilized it never occurred to the men to hack through that curtain of privacy, not before confirming absolutely that this was a derelict. Fehd put his hands on some of them, as if he could learn something by touch. He was practically licking his lips at the thought of what riches those crates might hold. Then again, they could just as easily contain shipments of underwear for a species long-dead, and then where would they be?

They moved cautiously—largely thanks to Burran, but Madaku had to admit that the ship's interior made him uneasy. Probably just the dire influence of the security specialist. Burran had suggested they send the ship's robot over, instead of live personnel, but he hadn't argued when Fehd said no. The presence of a mere robot would not constitute a salvage claim, and if there were any survivors aboard it could create a legally fuzzy situation, wherein the robot could be considered as forfeited to *Ironheart*'s occupants. More importantly, there were at least twenty major cultures, human and non-, that considered humanoid robots an abomination, and sending one unasked aboard their ships was one of the few ways left to spark a violent confrontation.

Of course, there were plenty of non-humanoid robot models out there. But Fehd had picked his up on the cheap. One of the few things Madaku and Burran were able to share a laugh over was the idea that the robot was, in fact, so cheap and shitty that the day they needed it, it would probably break down. But that was only a joke—the odds of anything breaking down on the *Canary* were vanishingly small, unless the ship were left derelict a few centuries as *Ironheart* had been. It had been a thousand years since the diagnostic and self-maintenance tech had become advanced enough that serious problems repaired themselves, even in bargain-basement second-hand shit.

They air-swam out of this first room. Their hands were free—all the readings they needed were displayed on the insides of their visors, and if a situation arose in which they needed weapons, their suits' AI's would activate its defenses and use them with better reflexes than the humans could ever manage. The firearms mag-clamped to their thighs were formalities more than anything else.

When they entered the corridor, it curved away to their left, their view obscured by the bend after twenty meters or so, but to their right it continued straight on for about forty meters before making a sharp left. Burran frowned: "Why should it be laid out so irregularly?" There were hatchways on both sides of the corridor, spaced an average of five meters apart but with noticeable variation. The hatches were not all the same make or color, and they all had different locking mechanisms. Some had no visible locking or latching mechanisms, at all.

They paused to take that in. One or two hatches might be replaced haphazardly in a ship's lifetime. But none of them had ever been on a vessel where it was impossible to tell which make of interior hatch was the original. Not only that, but the hatches were such different sizes that it looked like the bulkhead must have been cut through in places to accommodate them. Wouldn't it have been much easier to order or manufacture hatches that fit the already existing specifications? Could the ship's interior parts have been intentionally mismatched, from the start?

They chose the curving path to the left. Not only did the tubular corridor curve, it also descended down deeper into the ship—they had been swimming along for many seconds before Madaku reminded himself that, in zero-G, one could just as easily say they were ascending as descending, yet he still could not shake the feeling that they were going down and not up. The walls were irregular, and the tunnel gradually narrowed. It was such a subtle change that it would have been on the mere edge of the range of human perception, except that their visor readouts kept them abreast of it. Along the walls were more crates, held in place by racks. There seemed to be no order to their placement or type. One of the crates was not really a crate at all—it looked to Madaku like a great box made of *clay*. He was finding the whole thing unsettling. There was no reason for a spaceship not to have a rational design; the fact that he couldn't make any sense of this one's bespoke some exotic alien intelligence unlike any he'd ever dealt with. Almost like the sort of legendary creatures that had supposedly roamed before the Hygienes.

On their left they came upon a doorway whose hatch stood open, leading into a big chamber. They floated into it, Madaku first. As he went over the threshold, Madaku spotted something that startled him, and he yelped and floundered in mid-air. Burran automatically yanked first Madaku, then Fehd behind him, placing himself between them and whatever the threat might be.

Only it didn't seem to be much of a threat, after all. Nevertheless, each man's breath grew faster. Even Burran's.

Across the room, in a transparent coffin, was a woman, propped up against the coffin's back. At this distance she was small; yet the sight of her was such a shock she seemed to fill the mind.

She had dark, nearly black hair; wavy, down to her shoulders. Her face was youngish—there was no telling what cosmetic treatments she may have had, but if she'd aged naturally she was probably around forty. Her oval face was well-proportioned, but her thin lips drooped down at the corners, and even in stasis her eyebrows seemed drawn together, giving her a severe expression. She had to be in stasis, and not dead or asleep. You could see the blood still pink under her sallow skin, despite the fact that her chest and diaphragm were completely motionless under her pinkish-gray unitard.

The three men hung back at the entryway, regaining their breath. It wasn't only their irrational fear of ghosts, zombies, and the like that had spooked them. A crewmember in suspended animation was the kind of thing that might be surrounded by defensive boobytraps. Burran scanned even more carefully than he had done so far.

Finally he said, "Looks safe," and began to swim toward the coffin.

Fehd hung back. "Are you sure?" he said. "Did you check for everything?"

"You can never check for *everything*, Fehd," Burran replied, mocking Fehd's remark from earlier, and continued on his way.

Madaku and Fehd swam across the room after him. "How long has she been there?" demanded Fehd. "Has she been in suspended animation ever since those thrusters started going cold?" Madaku couldn't decide whether the intensity of Fehd's tone came from his aggrievement at having his salvage rights snatched away by a survivor, or by amazement at the ship's suspended-animation tech. Probably amazement, he decided. Credits were nice, but it wasn't like anyone was ever likely to have so few they'd go hungry. But tech like this would be genuinely exciting.

Neither Burran nor Madaku acknowledged Fehd's question, since they had no way of answering it yet. As they neared the coffin, Madaku started to say, "First thing, let's see if we can figure out the readouts. If it's been such a long hibernation, there could be complications during the revival...."

His words cut off with a gasp. They all gasped, not just him.

The woman's eyes had popped open. Not a groggy, slow, blinking journey back into wakefulness. They snapped open, spent a millisecond roving around the chamber, then returned to the three arrivals and moved back and forth among them, fixing on first one and then another.

"Her chest isn't moving," said Fehd. With a chill, Madaku realized Fehd was right. She also didn't seem to be blinking. Fehd pulled the doctor off Madaku's thigh. He pointed it at the woman and started scanning.

"What's it say?" asked Burran.

Fehd shook his head at the readings. He seemed to be using the doctor as an excuse not to have to raise his eyes to the eerie woman in the transparent coffin. "Just, she's, uh, she's coming out of suspension. Vitals still very low."

"I can see that," said Burran, "because her chest isn't moving. So why is she awake?"

"Maybe it's, um, maybe it's just a reflex," said Fehd.

Burran snorted.

Right now the woman was looking straight into Madaku's eyes. He said, "That's not a reflex."

Her eyes bore into him—no muscle of her body seemed to have moved except for those controlling her eyes. Madaku found her expression and the thoughts behind it inscrutable, but he was certain there was a wakeful awareness behind those eyes.

Her gaze continued to move from one to the other of them. They didn't dart back and forth in confusion. They went from one to the other at a slow, steady pace, as if she were evaluating them, summing them up from her distant, aloof vantage.

"Yeah," said Burran. "Madaku's right. She sees us."

Four

Fehd was scanning her with the doctor and shaking his head.

"What is it?" Madaku demanded.

"Her brain's back on, but it's way ahead of her body."

"So she's got a suspended animation chamber that works on different principles than the ones we know," said Burran. Madaku held his tongue, reflecting that Burran probably didn't understand just how radically different those principles would have to be.

Whatever the readouts Fehd was staring at said, it must have been pretty damn interesting to have ripped his attention away from the woman herself, and her cold glare. Frowning at the doctor's screen, he said, "Her brainwaves are weird. The doctor can't diagnose it, or come up with any theories on what it means, but they're weird."

"But she's human, right?" said Burran.

"Uh, yeah. Almost definitely."

The woman's chest and diaphragm began to move. She pushed a button set into the wall of her coffin, and the men began to drift to the floor as the artificial gravity cranked back on. It was a slow descent, and they had time to orient themselves so that they landed comfortably with their feet on the floor, standing before the coffin. The gravity was heavier than what they maintained on the *Canary*, but as cosmopolitan prospectors they were accustomed to a range of gravities.

They tried not to fidget as she pressed another button and they heard the hiss of her coffin unsealing. It was ridiculous for them to be the nervous ones—the woman was the one waking

31

up all alone after who knew how many centuries, surrounded by three strangers.

Then again, they'd only assumed she was all alone. It might not be a fluke that her suspended animation coffin had kept working so long, and there might be other crewmembers sprinkled throughout the ship, waking up now. Their readings hadn't picked up any, but they hadn't picked up this woman, either.

Even lying there prone and silent, she had such a strange air of confidence about her; there was a quality to her that Madaku had never quite seen. It took him a long moment to find the proper words to describe it, because they were words which had passed out of active use in all the cultures he'd lived in: words like stately, and regal.

The lid of the coffin raised itself. The movement was accompanied by a chime, a little touch Madaku had never come across. Not that he'd seen more than a couple dozen suspended animation chambers. When you could zip across the whole galaxy in the space of a few months, thanks to hyperspace jumps, there wasn't much need for suspended animation.

The straps that had held the woman in place during the long centuries of zero-G unwrapped themselves and snapped back inside the coffin's interior walls. Madaku thought that he'd like to get a closer look at some of that tech, and at some of this circuitry that seemed immune to entropy. Then the woman was stepping out of the coffin, and Madaku stopped caring about the circuitry.

She held herself erect, her posture perfect. Each foot landed perfectly as she took three steps. By rights she should have been groggy, confused, clumsy as her body tried to shake off the long, accumulated inertia, as her mind tried to plug itself back in. But there was no hint she'd had so much as a brief nap.

It was Burran she moved toward. Halting before him, she said, "Art thou the leader?," in a clear strong voice with no cracks from disuse.

Burran paused a tad longer than this straightforward question called for. Madaku noted the way Fehd bounced on his toes in annoyance at the delay. He wondered if Burran's hesitation came from a desire to needle Fehd a little, or from a genuine unwillingness to admit that he wasn't the leader.

When Fehd was on the verge of taking it upon himself to answer, Burran finally jerked his head the other man's way and said, "Nah, that'd be this guy."

The woman looked at Fehd with a glimmer of what Madaku thought might have been surprise, if she'd deigned to be interested enough to feel anything as strong as surprise. "Ah," she said. "It was thy boarding of the vessel that awakened me."

"Yes," said Fehd, then kept opening his mouth to say something else, but let each syllable die unborn on his lips, unable to come up with the appropriate words. The expected thing would have been gratitude, but the woman sounded almost reproachful. "I … I hope you don't mind?..." said Fehd, at last.

"Of course I do not. One must sleep. But then, one must awaken." She again surveyed them all, and said, "You may remove your helmets. The air of *Ironheart* shall not corrupt the lungs."

When they didn't obey right away, the woman raised an eyebrow. For some reason, that was enough to get them reaching for their release toggles. Even Burran, though he made a show of first double-checking the readings on the atmosphere.

The woman turned back to Fehd. "Is this thy crew entire?"

"Three-fourths. The pilot's back on our own ship. I'm Fehd. This is Burran—he does security, mainly. And that's Madaku. He's engineering, for the most part."

"Have you no other names?" she said. "No ranks?"

The three men exchanged looks. There were still a few human societies that used surnames, but galaxy-wide they had been rare a hell of a long time. No matter how long she'd been asleep, it was bizarre for this woman to be surprised that they didn't use them.

Fehd explained the custom that had been popular for the last couple thousand years: "We all come from cultures that don't particularly care about genetic kinship, so there's no need for family surnames. As for rank, I mean, if someone wants to refer to me in some specific capacity, they just call me Fehd Captain. Or Fehd Ship-Proprietor. Or Fehd Prospector."

Burran put in, "And if there's a bigger ship with a large crew divided into sections with hierarchies, you just specify their place in the hierarchy. Like if Madaku here was part of a big ship with forty engineering personnel, you could call him Madaku Engineer Thirty-five, or something like that."

"Or Madaku Engineer One, possibly," said Madaku.

The woman took them all in, her gaze on them but simultaneously on some other distant point, perhaps somewhere deep within, perhaps someplace out in the empty vastness. "I see," she said, as if putting aside something that had briefly seemed interesting but had proven easily classifiable, after all. "There has been a leveling."

"What's your name, by the way?" said Burran.

"I am Anya Molina Escobar de Bucchio Pendergast-Fallon."

"Quite a name," said Burran wryly. As a matter of course he'd fed the name into his tablet while she spoke. "Pretty unusual to boot. There's no record in the Registry of anyone having used that exact name in six thousand years—congrats. How about your Registry code?"

"I have no code in the Registry."

They stared at her even more intensely. She seemed unfazed by the attention. Madaku said, "Ma'am, with all due respect. Anyone who's had any dealings with government or commerce in the last five thousand years, on anything but a strictly local scale, has been assigned a code in the Galactic Registry."

"I've had no such dealings," she said, her eyes roaming over the chamber's interior, as if she'd gleaned everything of interest from the intruders and was now interested only in making sure her ship was in proper shape.

Fehd pressed the point: "You haven't bought anything at anyplace bigger than a planetside or intra-system market? You haven't dealt with a government agency at anything greater than the planetary level?"

"My needs are few," she said.

The men kept silent. None of them quite believed her, but they saw no reason to contradict her yet.

And, as they listened to the old-fashioned Galactic roll from her mouth, they couldn't help but think, *Who knows?*...

Turning to Fehd, she said, "I should like to visit thy ship. I assume thy instruments may confirm I carry no weapons or diseases?"

"Sure," said Fehd. From his eagerness, his two companions could predict what he was going to say next: "And perhaps later we could explore your ship, as well. I'd love to learn *Ironheart's* secrets." He was practically drooling over the prospect of getting his hands on that suspended animation technology.

Anya said, "Some of her secrets I may share, perhaps. And some I must keep."

Madaku noted the very, very antiquated affectation of giving a vessel the female pronoun. He had never heard anyone do that in real life, and knew the custom only from classical literature he'd had to study in school.

Anya said, "Let us depart for thy vessel," and began leading the way out of the room.

Without thinking, Fehd and Madaku fell in step behind her. When Burran exclaimed, "Wait!" they were startled. Anya, on the other hand, merely stopped and turned a mild, questioning gaze on him.

Burran said, "You mind telling us what happened to your ship, before we go traipsing over to ours? Mind telling us whether you had any other crew in here, and if so what happened to them?"

"I've no objection to telling thee whatever thou may wish," she said, perfectly reasonable. "When the last sleep came, I was alone. It is a very long time since *Ironheart* has held *crew*, as such, though I have at times had companions. As to what happened to her, I know not exactly." At first Madaku wondered who "her"

35

referred to, and assumed it was one of those companions. Then he realized she meant the ship itself. "I came upon this system, and when I wanted to leave, the engines would not go. Being only myself, and having no engineer with me, I could not repair it. So I settled in to sleep, trusting that ones such as you would come awake me, in time."

"Who intuited you out here? Are you the intuiter?"

"The person who was with me took her life. The frame of her spirit buckled under the weight of the void."

Shit, a ship really would be in trouble if its intuiter up and killed herself. And if that subspace antenna had been knocked out before the accident, that would explain why Anya hadn't called for help. There were still a lot of questions, but the sadness in Anya's voice made the men shy, and they dropped the subject for now. "Madaku here will be happy to look over your thrusters, see if he can get them running again," said Fehd. Another chance to pick up some marketable titbits, naturally.

Burran said, "What did you come here for, anyway? Were you mining?"

For the first time Anya showed something like amusement in the lightness of her lips. "Nay," she said. "*Ironheart* contains riches enough."

Madaku would have liked a moment alone with Burran to discuss things before carting the stranger over to the *Canary*. If *Ironheart* had such fabulous riches, how come Anya hadn't had an engineer on the payroll, way back when? Or a killer diagnostic system? And what the hell had she been doing way the hell out here at XB-79853-D7-4, anyway, if she hadn't been here to mine? Not counting its mineral wealth, the place was so desolate that not even zyblots wanted to live here, as they had so amply and needlessly proven.

But Fehd seemed only to have heard, firstly, Anya confirming that she had registered no rival prospecting claims that would precede his, and, secondly, that her ship contained a large amount of wealth. After that, he couldn't get her back to the shuttle and then the *Canary* fast enough.

Madaku was hoping she might lead them on some circuitous route back to the docking bay, perhaps leave this chamber by a different door, and so give them a chance to see another part of the ship. He was curious to try to gauge how big the habitable area might be, and to see if the rest of the craft's interior was designed in such a seemingly haphazard fashion. But she led them back the way they'd come. It took less than a minute, now that they were briskly walking instead of cautiously air-swimming.

"This ship has an interesting design, Anya," he said to her as they walked. "Has it been modified much since you took possession?"

She didn't slow her pace as she answered, but she did turn her head to speak over her shoulder. "Modifications have been made, here and there. Over the years, I trust that every part hath been replaced, except the outer central hull."

Every part? More exaggeration. "Where did you first acquire it? If I may ask. Is it a human design, at least originally?"

Anya kept walking. For a moment, he didn't think she was going to answer. But then she said, uncertainly, "I don't remember."

Madaku and Burran exchanged a look. Not remember where you bought your starship? Bullshit. But bullshit so flagrant as to give one pause. Madaku began to ask himself if this Anya might not be clinically insane, and what they would do about it if she were. No sane person should be able to nonchalantly claim such a lapse in memory.

They boarded the shuttle; the craft undocked itself and began the quiet trip back to the *Canary*. Anya cast her black eyes around its interior, taking stock. But she showed only a lukewarm interest. Madaku didn't blame her much. Even if she had gone to sleep millennia before this particular model was ever produced, still, a shuttle is a shuttle.

Willa had been following their adventures remotely. Now Burran inclined his head as a mild buzzing in his earpiece threaded through the cabin of the shuttle, on the edge of the audible. Of course it could be no one except Willa, but Madaku nevertheless imagined he could have identified the sound of Willa's voice just from that faint thin buzz, that he would have recognized it even without knowing already who it was; of course that probably wasn't true.

To Fehd, Burran said, "Willa wants to know if she should do anything special to welcome our guest."

Fehd turned to Anya. "Um, if there's something you'd like?...."

She didn't take her eyes from the viewport, and from the quickly swelling *Canary*. "I want only to be surprised," she said.

While Fehd was trying to think of what to do with that cryptic answer, Burran said, "Willa? Don't worry—no need to do anything."

Madaku watched him, annoyed. Really, it should be the captain who stayed in touch with the pilot, but because of their special relationship Fehd let Burran do it. Madaku didn't think it was wise to indulge their romance to the point that it encouraged unprofessional behavior.

The *Canary* was above them now, as they went under its belly in order to get to the docking area on its other side. Anya craned her neck to look up at it, as it passed overhead. "'Tis a fat ship," she said; disapprovingly, as if it were a beast bred for display, instead of a machine designed to certain specifications for certain reasons.

"It's not a *fat* ship," Fehd said defensively. "It's a mining ship. That's the hold you're looking at."

"Mm," said Anya, as if Fehd's mitigating circumstances left her unimpressed. "So thou shalt fill that great hold with crushed moonlets?"

"Yeah," said Fehd. "Pretty much."

"Like a swollen tick," Anya murmured, possibly to herself. None of the men knew what a tick was, and they let the comment go. It didn't sound like a compliment.

Madaku cleared his throat. He didn't know why it should make him a little nervous to address the newcomer. "I'll have to research the pronoun usage, Anya," he said. "I can't remember when to use words like 'thou' and 'thy' instead of 'you.' It's a long time since school. I think the 'you' is for plurals, and to show respect to individuals?..." He blushed after having said the last bit, as he realized that Anya had not been calling any of them "you" individually.

Madaku didn't really care about the pronouns, he was just trying to get a conversation started, to see what else he could pick up about her. But at first, it once again seemed that she might not say anything; when she did speak, it was to say, "Nay, it is not for you to learn my dead speech. That task is mine. Always, when one awakens, there is a new tongue to learn. On the one side, one regrets making such effort for such a paltry, quickly-'scaping end. To learn a speech that will be less than a memory to those one must speak to upon the next awakening! But on the other side, 'tis good to have a little task, and one is always grateful, upon awakening, to discover there is at least one thing one must do."

Fehd asked, "Um, are you saying that it's happened to you multiple times that you've gone into suspended animation for so long that, when you awoke, the lingua franca had shifted significantly? How many times have you used the suspension chamber? How old is it? What kind of maintenance do you do?"

They were coming up the other side of the *Canary* now. Its hull scrolled by, illuminated by the shuttle's running lights and the faint reflected aquamarine light of XB-79853-D7-4. Anya said, "The change this time is not so great; I shall be able to ape thy speech in short order. A difference in accent, in a few words. But so little has changed in so long—thy technology looks much as it looked when last I went to sleep. There has been a leveling, true. But I have seen levelings afore."

Fehd wasn't sure what to say to all of that. "Well," he tried, "if it's a concern, I'm sure we can coach you on how to speak more like, you know, us."

"You should let Willa be in charge of that," said Burran. "She's good at that stuff. Teaching. Explaining."

Anya turned away from the *Canary's* constantly-tumbling hull, to look at Fehd. "Thou hast asked many questions about my suspended animation unit. Doth my technology interest thee?"

Fehd's mouth opened and closed several times, without finding an answer he liked. A better businessman would have downplayed his interest in the newcomer's goods. But despite Fehd's pretensions and daydreams, it had been many centuries since anyone in Galactic society had truly had to make a living from haggling, so it was no surprise he wasn't better at it.

Finally, Fehd gave up. "Yes," he said. "I'd like a chance to look it over." Anya slowly turned to look back out at the *Canary*.

Instead of holding firm in the face of her silence, Fehd quavered, "I'm sure we can find a way to make any disclosures worth your while."

Anya was still looking at the ship. Madaku was getting used to her stately pace in answering. Her pauses made her eventual replies something to look forward to, somehow.

When she did reply, she said, "Yes, we shall see—thou mayest have something I desire."

Five

When they boarded the *Canary*, they got to see a new side of Anya. Willa was waiting in the docking bay to meet them. She eyed the stranger with friendly curiosity—but whatever friendliness she might display was more than outdone by the almost gushy way Anya stepped forward, took both her hands, and said, "But thou art *charming!*"

"Well, thanks!" said Willa, laughing in delight.

Anya turned her body in the men's direction, without actually tearing her eyes from Willa. "This is the one you said shouldst teach me your speech, yes?" Fehd nodded, and Burran merely grunted in reply—they'd already told Anya the *Canary* had a complement of only four, so who else would it be? Anya went on: "She must teach me in matters of speech, and also in all things else."

Fehd said, "Well, sure. Willa, you don't mind, do you?"

Willa glanced at Burran; Madaku intercepted the look. At first he took it for a silent request for permission, and his blood began to boil; but then he recognized it for what it was, a reassurance. That struck him as even odder. He looked at Burran to see what expression he gave Willa in return, but it was unreadably stoic.

For the next couple days Willa mainly just hung out with Anya. There wasn't a lot else for her to do—normally, she would have helped the others out in getting the extraction and exploitation-chains set up, but those activities were so far outside her area of expertise that she would only have been good for odd jobs here and there, and the guys were able to pick up the slack. Besides, Fehd liked it that Willa was keeping

Anya distracted from all the profitable activities going on in this system that Anya had, after all, visited first.

It was a lot of work for three people, getting a mining operation set up for a whole solar system, even if their main focus was only XB-79853-D7-4 and its cloud of satellites. So they had to leave Willa and Anya on their own most of the time. At the end of the day or the beginning, before or after work, whenever Madaku walked into a room occupied only by Anya and Willa, he was amazed at the vast difference between the face she showed the intuiter and the one she gave the rest of the crew. With Willa she was like an adoring sister, usually older but sometimes seeming younger, like a child gazing up at Willa in worshipful admiration. There was something a little extreme about it, actually.

With the other three, Anya continued to comport herself almost as a queen. But Willa's influence did soften her. Sometimes, if Willa was also in the room, the men might find turned upon them the still-warm remnants of a smile originally ignited for Willa's sake. And Willa seemed to like Anya too, albeit with far less intensity.

One day while they were working side-by-side, Madaku said to Burran, "So—what do you think of the relationship developing between Willa and Anya?" He asked partly out of spite, because he could see that Burran didn't like it. Presumably that was because it occupied time Willa would normally devote to him.

But Burran gave no hint of any personal jealousy when he replied. Predictably, he was concerned with security. "I don't know if it's a good idea to have Willa answering any questions our mysterious stranger can think of to ask about us, sixteen hours a day."

Madaku was certain that, however Burran might dress it up in his own mind, the truth was he was jealous. No one could be as paranoid as he seemed to be. "You're the one who suggested Anya be assigned to Willa."

"For language lessons. How long does it take to teach her to say 'you' instead of 'thou'?"

Madaku had to admit that Burran made a good point, even if he only admitted it to himself. Fortunately, Anya would be at least somewhat separated from Willa soon. After the fourth day of setting up asteroid stations for the extraction chains, and getting the preliminary infrastructure set up for the exploitation chain, Fehd figured he could let Madaku coast a while. There would be some time for Madaku to go over to *Ironheart* and try to help Anya get it up and running again (and, incidentally, see if he could pick up on any valuable tech quirks or innovations it might harbor). Burran's workload was lighter now, too, and Fehd told Madaku that getting Anya away from Willa would also be a nice way for the couple to have some time alone.

And Madaku had his own secret project that he wanted to work on. It intrigued him, it almost galled him, that Anya's code was not available in the Registry. During his off-hours he'd found himself poring over the samples of it they'd cloned and uploaded to the Registry and placed in the *Canary* AI for analysis. It was confirmed that the Registry had never heard of it or anything obviously related to it. Almost as if there had been a whole independent cybernetic culture out there, some race of computer-savvy sentients, that had gone extinct and left no trace of their mathematical techniques or programming strategies except the code on *Ironheart*. Undoubtedly the explanation was nothing so dramatic as that, but it remained an intriguing problem, and Madaku found himself fiddling with it more and more obsessively. He welcomed the prospect of being invited to deal with her code still more. Who knew, maybe he would figure out a way to hack into it—purely as an intellectual exercise, of course, with no invasive intentions.

So Madaku and Anya boarded the box-like, utilitarian shuttle and headed back over toward *Ironheart*.

It gave Madaku the willies, being alone with Anya. Exposure to Willa had mellowed her, but a lot of that softening disappeared along with her tutor. During the ride back to her ship, there wasn't much small talk. When they were about halfway over, Madaku gave it a shot: "Will it be good to get back to your ship?"

There was her habitual pause before answering. She was sitting behind Madaku, gazing out at the starfield. Though she leaned far back in her chair with her legs wide, not even a casual observer could have thought she was slumping, or accused her of lazy posture. By leaning back and spreading her legs out, she gave herself the illusion of more mass, more volume. Though her hands curled light and loose atop her thighs, energy thrummed through her body. Sometimes he imagined he could feel the maddened electrons popping off her and hitting him.

Finally, she said, "One always returns. That is the way things are. But it is important that things be made new, as well. Or, at least, that one try to make them so."

That didn't exactly make sense, but whatever. "Well, I'll take a crack at it. Even if your engines are unfamiliar to me, the Registry will come up with similar models, and we'll soon have you good as new." Hesitantly, as if asking too many questions would be presuming too far upon the privilege of this audience, he said, "How long have you owned *Ironheart*?"

Anya had looked away from *Ironheart* and seemed to be examining the stars to remind herself which ones she had visited and which ones she had yet to see. "Did I not tell you?" she said. "I do not remember."

"You told me. I guess I thought maybe it was a temporary lapse caused by the effects of suspended animation." It seemed to him that at the mention of suspended animation a mysterious, cold amusement flickered briefly in her face.

Ironheart's slowly turning thruster-wings were near enough to make out their inscriptions with the naked eye. Madaku remarked how alien so many of them seemed, how old. He said, "May I ask how you got so many names, Anya?"

Her vision pierced into some hidden, phantasmagorical place, and one could almost see her repeating to herself old tales of how she'd come by her many names. "I picked them up," she said. "Here and there."

They didn't say anything else till they arrived at her ship. Madaku could have asked Anya for an access code, but unless she offered it he decided to see if it was any easier to dock this time. Between what he and the AI had learned about *Ironheart*'s code when they'd docked four days ago, and the work he'd been secretly doing on the code in his spare time, they were able to dock. But the code had already mutated since their last visit, enough that again it took the shuttle's AI a second to persuade the airlock to open.

"How easily you broke my ship's defenses," observed Anya, while they waited for the airlock to pressurize. She didn't sound particularly upset—perhaps only the mildest exasperation.

"I hope you don't mind my accessing without asking first."

Anya said, "It does not matter. It is the way. Ever one awakes and finds that certain of one's tools are useless and must be replaced. Though that happens less and less. There was a time, I think, when one had to cycle through all one's possessions even without a sleep, even in the span of a normal life."

"Your defenses system put up a good fight," said Madaku. "The code's evolutionary morphing capacities are really pretty extraordinary. And it's so unusual that, even now that our AI has deciphered its core architecture and mutative principles, it takes the Registry almost a second to construct a key."

Anya gave him a sharp look. Madaku almost physically recoiled. She said, "One second? Dost thou speak to me of one second as if it might be an advantage in combat, in defense?"

Madaku wondered if she'd reverted to Classical Galactic because she was pissed off and not thinking, or if it was because she wanted to signal her contempt by using the second-person-singular on him. But why the contempt? What had he done? Almost stammering, he said, "Well, I guess I didn't mean it necessarily gave you a strong real-world advantage, or anything. But it's still an interesting, impressive bit of programming. And there are really ingenious defenses against anyone being able to hijack your system without your knowledge."

Anya ignored the second part of his statement. Her narrowed eyes lingered on him, feeling him out. "'Impressive.' You mean, as in a game?"

"Well. Um. Kind of, I guess."

Mercifully, after another moment, Anya took those eyes off him. As she turned to stride through the airlock and into the ship, Madaku hurrying after her, he heard her mutter, presumably to herself, "A world of low-stakes games—so be it, I've awoken in such as these before, as well."

They bypassed the room with the suspension coffin that Fehd was lusting after, and went straight to the bridge. Even so, Madaku saw enough to appreciate anew how bizarre *Ironheart's* layout was. It was impossible to see what had motivated the engineers to place the corridor's turns where they had, and everywhere there were those mysterious crates made from all different materials, held in racks along the walls. In places little nooks and niches had been carved into the bulkhead itself, and idols or trinkets or statuettes or trophies hid within their shadows—Anya maintained too brisk a pace for Madaku to pause and get a good look at any of them.

When they arrived at the bridge, Madaku saw that it had a much more old-fashioned set-up than the bridge on the *Canary*, or any other ship Madaku had ever stepped foot on. Most bridges were just conference rooms, since cybernetic redundancies meant that any command, action, or reading could be made from any terminal aboard or connected to the ship.

On *Ironheart*, though, important functions really were wired through the bridge. Madaku didn't see why it had been designed like that; it struck him as inefficient and dangerous. And, while the circuitry was very old, and the original unmodified base probably the oldest cybernetic set-up he'd ever seen, it wasn't so old that modern redundancies couldn't have been built in. It was as if it dated from an age when the minds of humans hadn't yet caught up with their technology, when they unthinkingly still designed their machines to be analogues with an animal, having this set of organs located in that specific place, having a brain centered in the bridge.

Anyway, that was why they had to actually physically go to the bridge, because that was where the controls for the scramblers were. Anya entered a code into a keypad that was fixed onto a console, so that it couldn't be moved around; then she underwent a retinal scan; then a tiny scraper popped out of the console, took an invisible sample of her skin cells, and ran a DNA test. Once the computer was satisfied Anya was herself, it allowed her to turn off the scramblers, so that Madaku could get a fuller look at the ship's inner workings and what had gone wrong with them.

The controls were marked in yet another script he'd never seen before, one made up entirely of squat triangles and rigid lines. The triangles and lines were arranged in all sorts of angles and clumps, diagonal lines cross-hatching, stacks of triangles tilted to the left or right. Eyeballing the consoles and readouts, Madaku guessed that he saw about a hundred characters, which would probably take it out of the running for being an alphabet and might mean they were part of a complicated set of ideograms. That was a significantly less efficient manner of writing, and was especially unusual in a ship's controls.

But whatever. Another weird thing, big deal. Who was counting anymore?

Madaku couldn't read the controls, obviously, and it would have been tiresome to have Anya translate everything for him, so he hooked his adapter up to her system.

Once the adapter's AI and the *Ironheart*'s had chatted a few nanoseconds, the adapter was able to show Madaku the ship's readings using the same format as aboard the *Canary*. He routed the data through a tablet, that he stretched out and propped up on his knees. Then he got to work.

He was hoping Anya would step out after she'd turned off the scramblers attached to her engineering sections and gotten the adapter hooked up. For one thing, her presence made him nervous, and for another it would be easier for him to snoop through the system, without her there watching him. Hooked up as he was to the system itself, from *Ironheart*'s own console and with permission of its master, he would break no Registry taboos in looking around.

But she didn't leave, she just sat in her black captain's chair and leaned it way back, and lounged there, gazing up at the tan perma-plastic ceiling. Madaku tried to ignore her, as he ran analysis protocols to figure out how the thrusters were supposed to work and diagnostics to figure out why they'd stopped working that way.

Before long, he was so caught up in exploring the information design, and solving the mystery of the engine failure, that he actually did forget Anya was there. So he jumped when she spoke.

"Tell me," she said. "If it was so easy for you to break my code's defenses and access my airlock, why could you not simply turn off my scramblers yourself?"

He was shocked and uncomfortable at the question, but tried to hide it. "We could have, of course. But we would never do such a thing without permission. Except, of course, in a true emergency."

For the first time, Anya looked taken aback. After taking a moment to let his words sink in, Anya said, "You mean you could have done all this without me? My scramblers are as weak to you as my airlock? You could have come onto the bridge, turned off the scramblers, and hooked up the adapter yourself, all while leaving me aboard your own ship?"

"Well ... yes, of course we *could* have." How could she not have figured this all out on her own? Even if she was from a time so distant that these things hadn't been true then—which, in truth, was a possibility that was only really hitting him now.... "We *could* have," he said. "But we never would. Except ... well, when first boarding we do have our AI turn off the scramblers for a nanosecond, with instructions to check only for survivors in need of assistance or immediate danger sources such as radiation leaks. Once the AI decides there's no such emergency, we switch off the view and re-enable scrambling before we can see anything else. Anyway, that all happens automatically, and only the AI gets to see that data—it's never shared with us." That had been moot in her ship's case, since the AI decay had rendered its data on the interior pre-scrambled, so to speak—although he had to admit that everything sure did seem to be functioning *now*, which was weird. Had her central AI rebooted itself?... He refrained from mentioning that there were, however, things that one could normally do in theory that did indeed seem hardly possible with *Ironheart*'s AI. For instance, the mutative rate prevented him from being able to create an interface sufficiently antibodied that *Ironheart*'s system would not recognize it; such an interface would have theoretically allowed him to manipulate her ship's systems without her or her AI realizing the commands came from an outside source. Naturally, such an action would be highly taboo and radically contra the Registry guidelines, and he would never consider actually doing it … but it was still weird that he *couldn't* do it.

The truth was that, in his spare time, he'd been trying to figure out if there were some way that he could. Not that he would—it was purely as a diversion.

She just kept staring at him. "Why do you switch off the view into the other ship?"

The longer her confusion lasted, the more discombobulated he became. "Well," he said. "To do otherwise would be incredibly impolite." Then he added, "And contrary to Registry Guidelines."

"Ah." Her expression showed the beginnings of comprehension, and amusement.

Madaku continued: "Obviously, when it's a question of boarding a ship that's possibly derelict, or possibly has someone aboard that needs to be rescued, in that case we're justified in boarding. But if we know it belongs to somebody, and especially if we're in contact with that owner, then it would take some pretty extreme circumstances to justify us forcing our way in and messing around with its systems...."

"Yes, yes, it all sounds very civilized." Nobody could have missed the amusement in her voice now. "You mentioned guidelines. Who is it that enforces these?"

Her question was so large and obvious that for a second he didn't understand it. Once it had processed, he said, "The Registry. You could make a complaint to the Registry, if we did that."

"I see." She reclined back in her chair again, and once more stared at the ceiling. Madaku hesitated, unsure whether they were finished. Then he returned his attention to the tablet on his knees, trying to regain his focus.

He worked for a while, studying the principles of Anya's thrusters, trying to look back in time and see why they had stopped working. There was no blaringly obvious reason. It looked almost like they'd been intentionally disabled. That was impossible, though, so he wondered if the problem hadn't been with the hyperdrive. In that case, he feared the ship would have much bigger problems than its realspace thrusters. But they'd need Willa to come over if they were to check that out. He began checking the hyperdrive couplings.

"Tell me," said Anya in a conversational tone behind him, "what would happen, if I killed you all?"

Madaku swiveled in his chair to face her. "Excuse me?"

Still reclined, she turned to face him. He saw that she was playing with something in her right hand—something like a toy, sort of like a little gray metal die except with prongs sticking out. Almost smiling, almost mocking him, she said, "Say that I upgrade my code. That I download more powerful code from the Galactic Registry. It sounds like all of you can hack into each other's systems whenever you like. Let us say I hacked into the *Canary*, lowered her energy shields from inside, and blasted her from the sky on a whim. What's to stop me from doing that, if your code offers such paltry protection?"

"Hopefully our first line of defense would be your total lack of desire to do anything remotely like that."

Again he could see her tightening with impatience. "Even if I've no reason to do it, dolt, there must still be those who would. There must be psychopaths, murderers, bandits. What happens if a shipful of nasty people came along and blew you up—what then?"

"The Registry would prosecute the attackers. The *Canary* and all its occupants are listed in the Registry, and the ship and we four crew members all have chips implanted, linked to our subspace antenna and sending signals to the Registry. If we should suffer sudden death or destruction, the Registry would immediately know of it. It would run a sweep through its contacts to see which of all its trillions were in the same vicinity as us. Once it did that, it would only take a little data-sifting for them to find the guilty party."

"You mean to say there are peacekeepers ready to swoop in to the remotest corners of the galaxy, each time there's a crime? That's absurd."

"The guilty party would be apprehended the first time they made contact with any community or group strong enough to do so. Otherwise that community or group would face censure by the Registry, for its inaction."

"But what is to stop these violent ones from avoiding all contact with any group? From coming to someplace, like, say, here, and living out the rest of their days in the wilderness of space?"

Now it was Madaku's turn to get impatient. "Well, yes, that does *happen*, but it's extremely rare! Too rare for us to go around constantly worrying about it. The fact is, most sentients like to at least sometimes be part of a community. There just aren't that many desperate individuals, within any given species.... I mean, maybe things were different before the Hygienes, I don't know."

Anya got that look again, like she was gazing into the distance of her inner self. "Ah, yes, the Hygiene," she said. "I remember that." Madaku thought that was a weird thing to say—anyone who'd ever been in school remembered hearing about the Hygienes. It was also odd that she said "the Hygiene," as if there'd been only one.

After she spent a while dwelling in wherever it was she went, Anya's eyes lost their haze and she turned to him. "I thank you for helping me see more clearly how things lie in this new world."

"Well, you know … no problem." Madaku had to keep reminding himself how long she'd been out. His latest analyses of the radiation trace-burns inside her thrusters suggested the engines had been cold for around six thousand years. Fehd might be hungry to see her suspension coffin so he could upload the design to the Registry, in exchange for credits. But Madaku wanted to see it, just so he could try to figure out how it worked. He'd double-checked with the Registry, and the longest anyone was ever on record as having spent in suspended animation was six hundred fifty-seven standard years.

Where had Anya's suspension coffin come from? It was that rarest of finds: something new. Madaku hadn't really wrapped his mind around it, but he had a feeling it might wind up being something truly momentous, merely because of that newness.

For now, though, he was worried about those hyperspace couplings. He couldn't think of what else could be wrong. While he was procrastinating about bringing the possible problem to her attention, she was off on another Civics-lesson tangent: "So tell me. When the Registry captures these people, these occasional murderers, what does it do with them? Make them an example? Publicly torture them and distribute the vids?"

"No—gods, no, of course not. The Registry enforcers feed them lotos and incarcerate them in one of the Wells of Melancholy."

Anya gave a little laugh. Madaku didn't see what was so funny.

Putting the tablet aside, he said, "I suppose the Registry didn't do that, when you last went to sleep?"

"Oh, no. The last I remember, the Galactic Registry was just that: a registry, where one uploaded news, facts, art, any data at all. It had pretensions to become the common ground of the galaxy but wasn't really there yet. Now, I see, it is. It was a gigantic server stored in hyperspace, whose realspace port was near Sagittarius."

"It still is. Well, the core is, anyway." He felt hushed before the notion that she dated from a time before the Registry was really the Registry. His gaze flickered around the old-fashioned bridge, its layout an echo from another culture. He said, "You … you're very old, aren't you?"

She looked straight at him with those eyes. He wasn't sure if he shuddered with his body, or if it was only in his mind. She gave him a faint, strange smile, one he would never be able to read, and said, "Oh, yes. I am very old."

Madaku swallowed. "How many times have you been in suspended animation?"

"Many times have I slept. I would not be able to count them all."

"Have you ever been out for as long as you were this last time? I mean, it seems like you were asleep for six thousand years."

"It is not the first time, no."

Madaku looked off into space, excited and frightened by the magnitude of it. "What was it like, back then? Back when you were awake?"

"The last time I was awake? Ah, the galaxy was a wild place then. The Registry was but a glorified newsfeed, and did no policing. A ship like *Ironheart*, if she wished, could destroy whole planets, then go on her way unhindered, or with a very good chance of being unhindered."

Madaku remembered how minutes ago, he had told Anya that what kept the number of murders down was that the bulk of people had an aversion to living out their days alone in an uninhabited wasteland. Now it occurred to him that, when her engines gave out, that may have been exactly what she was doing.

She went on: "Aye, it seems I did underestimate the Registry, even after having seen the wondrous violence it could wreak."

"Beg pardon? What's less violent than the Registry? It's been the foundation of peace for millennia."

"Yes, and I know upon what violent ground such peace is built. Think you the Registry grew strong so as to contain the Hygiene? Say rather the Registry follows the Hygiene as a rose grows from a seed, or rather that it fed on it as a maggot battens upon a corpse. There was the Registry even before the Hygiene, you know. But it was weak, a mere commodity serving the pleasure of unruly masters. It must have taken the Hygiene to make those masters long for the peace it offered. Ah, many are the worlds upon which I have caroused, that are naught but cinders now!"

"Wait, wait, wait. Are you saying that you remember from *before the Hygienes?*"

She tilted her head and pierced her dark eyes all the way through him, as if his stupidity had not quite yet ceased to amuse and exasperate her. "Do you not know already that I have been asleep six thousand years? And did I not just say this was not the first time I have slept so long?"

"I ... yes, I guess it makes sense, it's just ... before the *Hygienes* ... before the *Registry....*"

Madaku saw her take note of his sudden, mysterious fear and smile.

She nodded at the tablet he had set aside and changed the subject. "Tell me about my ship."

Madaku cleared his throat. "Yes, well." He picked up the tablet and looked at the readouts. "Lots of the realspace readings are puzzling, to be honest." Anya's face remained impassive at this; it was impossible to tell if his words surprised her, or not. He went on: "I have a hard time seeing what's gone wrong with the thrusters, and why whatever it is hasn't interfered with workings in the rest of the ship.... I'm worried there may be a problem with the hyperspace couplings."

"What sort of problem?"

"One of the couplings may be starting to decay. All the realspace portions of the ship seem to have held up well, but there might be some erosion of the hyperface."

Anya's mouth formed a grim shape. "When last I was awake, it was impossible to reattach a hyperdrive that had slipped its mooring. Is that yet true?"

"Yeah, afraid so. It's a math thing, it doesn't change. Even if it's just one coupling and all the others are still holding, once the coupling gives out, the piece of the hyperdrive it connects to in hyperspace will spontaneously morph and distort, and pass out of our reach."

"Then we must repair the coupling before it slips."

"Understand that I'll need Willa even to confirm that the problem exists. If it does, we can more or less fix it. But it'll never be possible to completely confirm that there's been no distortion in the hyperdrive. Normally, with this kind of damage and decay, it's safer to scrap the ship and get a new one."

"We must repair the coupling. *Ironheart* must fly. She must fly forever." She said this with great intensity, almost menacingly, as if it were she herself they were talking about.

"Well," said Madaku, returning to his tablet. He almost pointed out that nothing lasts forever, but something made him think better of it. "Like I said, even confirming the problem will need some hyperface work, and that means Willa. We'll need to get her over here, familiarize her with the equipment."

"Ah." Anya leaned back, all smiles now that Willa had been mentioned. "That shall be very fine."

"Meanwhile I'll keep running tests to see if I can come up with any other reason the realspace thrusters might have failed."

Anya nodded, as if she were bored now with the discussion. She stood. "You shall continue to work," she said. "I have items I wish to tend to." And she strode out of the bridge, shutting the door behind her.

Madaku breathed a sigh of relief to have her gone, even as he wondered about those "items." He returned his attention to the engineering problems. What he hadn't mentioned to Anya was that Fehd (and, unofficially but very possibly, Burran) would have to give Willa permission to come work on a craft other than the one she was contracted for. Not to mention that *Ironheart* would need an intuiter to get to the nearest repair community, and the *Canary* couldn't spare theirs.

Again he wondered: Why had the *Ironheart*'s intuiter killed herself, all those thousands of years ago?

Six

Anya told Madaku that she preferred to remain on *Ironheart* for a day or two, and that she would send a message when she wished to return. He wondered why she wanted to stay aboard the ship (tending to those mysterious items of hers?), and he bristled at her assumption that he would drop his work and come fetch her whenever she called. But it would give the crew of the *Canary* a chance to discuss the situation without Anya there. So he nodded and did as she said.

Back aboard the *Canary* he called a meeting in the Discussion Room. He had been right that Fehd would rub his chin and hem and haw at the suggestion that Willa be sent over to work with *Ironheart*'s hyperface to repair its coupling, pro bono. But he'd been wrong that Burran would oppose it, and it was soon plain why. As Fehd was just beginning to talk about how it really wouldn't be fair of Anya to expect such a valuable, vital service in exchange for nothing at all, Burran watched Willa with amused anticipation. Sure enough, she interrupted Fehd as he was saying, "Well, now, let's think about this," and made it plain that she found the idea of withholding such a service indecent and immoral, and possibly contra Registry guidelines. Fehd quickly backpedaled, protesting that he had never intended not to let her go over.

After the meeting adjourned Madaku stayed in the room to work on something on his tablet, and Willa hung back too.

"You've got a secret," she said, once they were alone.

Madaku began to stammer; then closed his mouth and, under her kind gaze, waited till he'd calmed down before speaking again. "It's disarming, how easily you see through me."

"I just look, that's all," she said. Madaku thought he caught a vague hint in her voice of a desire to correct him, to point out that it wasn't just *him* she watched, that there was nothing particularly special or personal about the attention she paid him. "Tell me what you're up to."

Embarrassed, he shrugged and said, "It's just this silly side project," but then he went ahead and told her. He hadn't stopped being intrigued by Anya's alien code; the Registry offered no direct guide to hacking it. Being able to take apart and rework her code had already presented a challenge by itself; and now that she'd mocked him for the ease with which he or anyone else could be destroyed by someone willing to live in isolation from Galactic society, he felt more encouraged than ever to figure the stuff out. Spurred on by that and the influence of Burran's mania for security, he'd started trying to design a transparent tendril, a line of code he could potentially slip into Anya's system, that would allow the *Canary* to observe and possibly even influence *Ironheart*'s operations. Basically a cheat, a way to make the invasive code invisible to the rest of the system even without being able to decipher *Ironheart*'s mutation principles and mutate fast enough to create code antibodies to protect itself from the ship's defenses.

Before he'd managed to explain very far, the seriousness of Willa's gaze unnerved him. Assuming it was due to her disapproval of his ethics, he hastened to reassure her: "It's only an intellectual exercise. Something to limber up my programming muscles. Nothing's going to come of it."

"No, I think it's a good thing," said Willa. That surprised him. "Let me know when you've cracked it. I'll tell the other guys what you're up to...."

"No, *please* don't. You don't understand, I'm not actually going to get anywhere, it's only a sort of game. It would take a true genius to quickly master code this different from the *Canary*'s. The details are too technical for me to really get into, but I've never even heard of anyone doing anything comparable."

"Madaku, if it would take a true genius to do this, then you'll just have to be a true genius." She reached up and squeezed his upper arm. The combination of her touch and hearing her say his name left him breathless. Did she know what she was doing to him? "I won't tell the guys, if that's what you prefer. But keep working at it, and let me know when you get somewhere. I have a feeling about Anya; I don't know, I think having a way in to her system might wind up being useful."

"Okay." Until now the tendril had been just a pastime. Now, though he still didn't believe he could succeed, he knew that it was going to become his main focus nevertheless.

Willa sent a message to Anya, saying she could come work on the coupling. Anya messaged back that Willa was most welcome and appreciated. Willa headed over on the shuttle within an hour after the meeting aboard the *Canary*.

There wasn't anything seriously wrong with the hyperspace coupling that Willa could find. Madaku was right that the realspace components showed signs of great wear, to a worrisome degree; but that was nothing Willa could handle from the hyperspace angle. Once she came out of the intuition bowl and finished crying, she told Anya that Madaku was just going to have to come back and take a closer look.

Meanwhile, she noted that Anya's hyperface was weird. It almost seemed like an auxiliary, smaller-scale hyperface—it gave access to the hyperdrive itself, sufficient for repairs and whatnot, but once plunged within it Willa's mind's eye could find no piloting portal. The bowl gave access to the engine, but not to the wider universe—that hyperface must be elsewhere. Willa wondered why it was set up that way. But instead of asking outright, she decided it might be interesting to see what Anya did, and did not, volunteer.

Anya insisted on having Willa stay over for a candlelight dinner. Willa messaged the *Canary* beforehand to let them know she was sleeping over; but first she messaged Burran privately, to let him know. He wasn't crazy about her staying. He insisted she at least leave the communicator on during dinner, but she gently refused. "That's rude," she said.

"Just don't tell her you've got it on."

"I don't know, baby. I get the feeling she would just be able to *tell*."

It would be wrong to say that Willa trusted her, but she didn't suspect Anya of wishing her harm. Anya and Willa were getting along quite well, in general.

But she knew Burran was right to worry. There was a reason people were trained in security, and a reason captains hired them for it. And she could sense that there was "something about" Anya.

She enjoyed the dinner, though she was a bit bemused by it. She'd never been to a candlelight dinner before, nor even heard of such a thing, though she knew that prehistoric people must have eaten and done most everything else by the light of raw fire.

They met in the dining room. Anya had given her directions from the quarters she'd assigned Willa for the night. When Willa arrived at the dining room, Anya was already there, and gestured to the place set for her at the ornate table, which looked like it was made from real wood and metals, and which was not huge but was a bit big for only two people. The walls, floor, and ceiling of the room were black, and it was dim because it really was lit only by candles. There were a fair bit of candles, though: five on the table, set in some sort of silver metal thing seemingly designed just to hold candles; and then more, set in doublets and triplets in sockets along the wall.

Once they were seated a squat and silent robo-butler came out and served them the soup course. The robo-butler was so old-fashioned and ancient, Willa wasn't sure whether it looked more like a toy or an antique. Either way, she was so delighted she nearly clapped her hands. Anya noticed how Willa was trying to follow along with her in choosing the silverware, and explained to her which was the soup spoon and gave her a quick run-down of the rules for all the rest of the cutlery. When Anya was done explaining Willa laughed and told her she'd probably have to go through the whole spiel again.

Anya smiled and said she didn't mind.

Conversation was slow at first, and restricted to Anya asking rather stiff questions about the other members of the *Canary*'s crew. Her speech patterns had become more contemporary under Willa's tutelage, though she did sometimes lapse back into her old pronoun usage, and she retained that stately rhythm. Willa, distracted by one of the burning wax-sticks' flickering, said, "Why are we eating by candlelight, by the way?"

"Ah. Well. I felt a celebration was appropriate. A celebration of how handily you confirmed *Ironheart*'s hyperdrive capacity. And, I hope, a celebration of the beginning of what shall prove to be a true friendship."

The answer struck Willa as a *non sequitur*, at first. Then she started to get it. "You mean the candles themselves are celebratory?"

Anya stared at her blankly, then burst into laughter. "Ah, all things do change, at long last! The notion of a 'candlelight dinner' as being special and set-apart was current for so long, I suppose I ceased even to think about it." Then she frowned, and when she spoke again it seemed she was talking to herself: "At least, I *think* the last time I was awake, people still did that. The last few times."

Willa waited, watching Anya disappear within herself. Then she asked, softly, "Anya, how old are you?"

Anya returned to her, and the present, with a smile. "Old. Very old. Older than you think!"

As a joke, Willa said, "Do you yourself even know, anymore?"

This time, the smile Anya gave in reply was so strange, Willa couldn't read it.

She returned to the candles: "Can you explain to me the ritual significance of these candles?"

"Oh, it's only a very vague one. Simply an extravagance. A way of showing a person that she, or he, is worthy of some trouble. And

I suppose that once, at the dawn of the electrical age, it must have been a means of hearkening back to an earlier, statelier time."

Willa laughed. "At the dawn of the electrical age! My, this custom stretches back all the way to our pre-human ancestors!"

Anya was still smiling, but she continued as if Willa hadn't spoken. "People like to ritually invoke earlier times, because they always believe the world was more civilized and less violent just a few generations go, or else more adventurous and romantic. But the differences are rarely so dramatic as all that."

The remark struck Willa as funny, because she'd grown up with the understanding that the Registry had long since done away with that old legendary large-scale violence, and that it was the galaxy of today which was the civilized one. She gazed at the candles on the tabletop until they imprinted negative blobs on her retinas, then turned to look at the more distant ones mounted on the walls. "They're very pretty."

"Ah. You've never seen a candle?"

"Never in real life. Only in history vids, fantasy vids."

"They're made of wax. Synthetic wax. There was a time when I insisted on having candles whose wax was made from real animal fat, but I've long since stopped caring."

Willa thought it was bizarre that Anya should specify that the wax was synthetic, as if it might have occurred to Willa it would be anything else. Something in her soul stirred in surprised horror at the idea of slaughtering a genuine living animal just to extract fat from it, when it would be vastly easier to get the fat from a protein matrix.

The soup course was done. The quaint robo-butler reappeared from its camouflaged niche, cleared their dishes, and set out the entrée. It appeared to be some sort of meat and some sort of vegetable. Willa began to eat, without asking any questions other than which cutlery to use. She hailed from a relatively cosmopolitan system, and had been exposed to enough recipes that nothing much struck her as exotic. And nothing dangerous would come out of a properly functioning protein matrix calibrated for humans.

Willa slowly chewed her food, as she weighed whether or not to broach the next subject. But the question seemed so blaringly obvious, that she couldn't see any point in pretending it wasn't on her mind. So she said, "Anya. May I ask why you came out here? To XB-79853-D7-4?"

"After the death of my companion, I sought desolation and loneliness."

Willa hesitated. "But wasn't your companion your intuiter? I assumed she ... I assumed you lost her after your arrival here."

"I'll tell you something you'll think extraordinary," said Anya, and leaned toward Willa across the table. "I didn't have an intuiter."

"You mean you're the intuiter?" She hadn't struck Willa as the type, and moreover it was mildly dangerous to have the intuiter be the only crew-member. When someone took off the intuition bowl and came out of the hyperface, they were in no condition to deal with any problems that might suddenly present themselves. Of course, it would probably be nothing the AI couldn't handle, but still.

But Anya said, "No. I am no intuiter. *Ironheart* has no need of one."

Willa made a dubious face, not wanting to be quite so rude as to openly doubt Anya, but not seeing any other choice. "With all due respect, Anya, there must have been an intuiter here. I mean, *Ironheart* wasn't built in the vicinity, was it? There aren't adequate facilities nearby, and never were. So somebody must have flown the ship out here."

Anya was nodding, like she'd heard all this before. She said, "This will be difficult for you to believe, but long ago I found a way to do without an intuiter, as you know it. Thus, I have long been able to live as the sole occupant of *Ironheart*, if I choose. Though it does grow lonely, traveling that way."

Willa squirmed. "Well. I don't mean to be rude. But, yeah, that's pretty hard to believe. People have been trying for thousands and thousands of years to figure out why the symbol logic of the human brain, and the other five pilot species, interacts so much better with the hyperscape than the symbol logic of AI's, or of the other sixty-three sentient non-pilot species. It's, like, one of the biggest philosophical, metaphysical problems of all time. Kind of every religion I've ever heard of talks about it. Really smart people have been trying to figure it out for all of Galactic history. And if you had a pure-cyber intuiter that would mean that you'd solved the riddle, right? You or whoever made the thing."

"And you wonder how it could be that I have found the answer when all those others have failed."

"Pretty much. Sorry."

"Do not apologize. The answer is simple. I once, very long ago, had the great good fortune to know an extremely intelligent member of a now-extinct species, who managed to solve the problem, and gave the solution only to me, shortly before he died. Shortly before the destruction of his planet, in fact. And now you have had the luck to randomly stumble upon me."

Willa stared at Anya, then laughed uneasily. "It's just too fantastic!"

Anya took a sip of her wine. "I am not offended by your incredulity."

"I mean, if you really have this device, then … like, could I see it? Because it would be the most amazing thing I ever saw."

"I disabled it."

"You disabled it? You had a thing like that, and you intentionally disabled it?"

"Yes. I disabled it, then shut down what systems still worked, then depressurized the ship. And went to sleep."

"But why?"

"Oh, Willa. I was very sad."

Willa blinked. What to say to that?

Anya's eyes were on her plate. She wasn't really eating at the moment, only moving food about with her fork. "As I have told you, there was someone else with me shortly before I arrived at this system."

For a moment she said nothing more. Willa remained silent too, keeping her eyes upon Anya.

Finally the strange woman resumed speaking. She said, "A woman who had traveled with me a long, long time. When she died, I wandered. Then I came here, and destroyed a component of the device I use for intuiting. I powered down the ship and went to sleep."

At last she gathered some food onto that fork, and raised her eyes to meet Willa's as she brought the morsel to her mouth. Willa met her gaze—compassionately, but withholding a part of herself. There were multiple things she felt to be true, and not all of them jibed together. The first was that, impossible though it might be, Anya truly believed that she had a means to hyperjump without need of an organic sentient intuiter; i.e., a pure-cyber intuiter. But the second thing was that this sad abridged tale she'd just recounted was true, too, at least in part: she'd had at least one crewmember aboard, around the time she'd come to XB-79853-D7-4. Presumably that had been her intuiter, and her death had been the reason Anya had been stranded out here. The trauma must have addled Anya's sense of the timeline, so that she believed the death had occurred before her arrival in the system—the grief must have triggered such quasi-suicidal despair that she misremembered herself as having chosen to put herself to sleep of her own volition, instead of from necessity. Who knew what strange effects grief and isolation might have on a lone traveler stranded at the very edge of the galaxy? For the moment Willa was concerned only with what Anya believed to be true, not with what objectively was.

The third thing was that Anya did not plan to harm her. Willa had no doubts about that. She herself, and not merely the package of skills she represented, had some intrinsic value to Anya—the woman practically radiated that truth. Willa didn't know if she would ever be able to actually use the fact to *influence* Anya, but she was certain she'd need not fear harm as long as she was aboard *Ironheart*.

65

With a sweet smile and a slight tilt of the head, she said, "Well, I'm very sorry, and I hope I haven't offended you. But much as I'd like to believe you, I can't." Hurriedly, she added, "I do believe that *you* believe it."

"Don't let it trouble you. I hope to have a chance to demonstrate it to you soon."

"I can tell you that if you really do have a machine that can pilot through hyperspace without a sentient pilot attached, every sentient in the galaxy will flip out the moment you upload it to the Registry."

But Anya said, "I have been considering showing it to Fehd. I know he has an interest in my gewgaws."

Plainly, Anya was a bit off. Even more fanciful than the notion that she might have such a revolutionary machine was the idea of just showing it to Fehd instead of uploading its specs to the Registry. Probably she had been stranded out here alone for a long long time after her intuiter had died, before she'd put herself into suspended animation. She'd started telling herself tall tales as a way of staving off insanity, and had wound up believing them just enough to go a little crazy.

Anya said, "Tell me of yourself."

"What would you like to know?"

"Tell me of the place you fill on the *Canary*. Are you happy there? Would you ever consider leaving?"

Uh-oh. "I would *consider* it, sure. I mean, Burran and I do have a contract with Fehd, and it's pretty specific about what conditions we're allowed to leave under."

Anya ignored all mention of the contract and focused on Burran. "Your lover. He would be among your conditions for taking a new post? That he should accompany you?" She sounded less than thrilled.

"First of all, I ought to point out that we're really not looking for a new ship." Poor Anya. For all her natural and legitimate dignity, there was something very sad about how she couldn't see what an unattractive prospect her crippled, ancient, musty, oddly labyrinthine ship would be for employment. It only made

66

Willa all the more tender. "But if we were, then, yeah, Burran and I would stick together. It would be awful for me to leave him, after all he's done for me. Anyway, I love him."

Anya studied her as she spoke. Dabbing her mouth with a napkin, she said, "Your crewmate Madaku thinks that your lover is a brute, and unworthy of you."

Willa's nerves flashed hot as thruster-tubes. "He said that to you?"

"Oh, no. He may never have said it to anybody. As one ages, one has less need to hear certain things said aloud."

"Oh. Okay. Well." Willa herself knew perfectly well that was what Madaku thought. Hearing it finally said openly was nonetheless unpleasant, though, and made it something more difficult for her to politely fail to notice.

It felt like Anya was looking more and more deeply into her, with no effort at all. As Willa met her calm, penetrating, unreadable gaze, she grew uncertain. For a crazy moment, Willa wondered if *she* was going crazy, because suddenly everything Anya had said seemed perfectly plausible. Why couldn't she have some sort of miraculous pure-cyber intuiter stashed away on board? She could have anything. "What's in all these crates that are stacked all over? And in all these small rooms? This ship is like a maze."

"Trinkets," said Anya. "Tell me what Burran has done for you. I don't mean to challenge you, I simply am curious."

If Burran had been in Willa's place, subjected to this sort of interview, he would have turned it around on Anya, would have wanted to know what her interest was in the crew's private lives and would have refused to divulge much information. Madaku and Fehd probably wouldn't have been so suspicious, but they would have found Anya's intensity gauche, and would have given only trivial answers. What Willa saw was a lonely woman of great independence and noble character, attempting to soothe her loneliness without suffering the indignity of admitting that was what she was doing. So she was happy to answer.

67

It was a big question, though. "He's done a lot for me," she said. "For one thing, he's the reason we're here, with the *Canary*. When Fehd put out the call for a new intuiter, Burran didn't try to talk me out of accepting or discourage me at all. Of course, technically it was a promotion for him, too, since Fehd agreed to bring him on as sole security officer. But obviously he was happier before."

"Where was that?"

"He was in charge of security in the Davenport System."

"Hm. Tell me, friend Willa. This new galaxy seems so very *safe*. Why then is there need of a security specialist, such as Burran?"

"Oh, well, you know. On a lot of ships like the *Canary*, it's almost just a formality to have one."

"Your Burran seems not to think it a mere formality."

"No, that's true, he doesn't." Willa made only a half-hearted attempt to muffle the pride in her voice. "Fehd got really lucky, actually. He was on the look-out for an intuiter and a security specialist, both, and he didn't want to spend too much. You've probably noticed how much Fehd likes a bargain. Anyway, the shares he was offering were more than enough for me—I'd never been a lone intuiter before. But it never would have been enough to afford Burran, if Burran hadn't been gung-ho enough on me taking this opportunity that he was willing to settle for a quarter the pay he had been getting."

"Curious. Is it not customary for an intuiter to get a larger share of mining profits, than the security specialist? It strikes me that the intuiter must be the most vital member of the crew."

"Yeah, all other things being equal. But, like I said, this is my first job as a solo intuiter. Before this I only ever worked in the short-range intuiters' bank in the Davenport System. Whereas Burran is one of the few security specialists with any experience worth a darn. He had to deal with real, actual violence sometimes. As Security head he was working on the surface of Davenport, in the reservation of the Shaggy Thwaps."

Naturally, Willa then had to explain to Anya the Shaggy Thwaps, a tribal species of humanoids native to Davenport. Their linguistic capacity was functional enough, albeit a bit lacking in abstracts, and they had a high enough intelligence to rate as sentients; but they weren't smart enough that they would ever independently develop any real technology, much less spaceflight. That was why they'd been spared by the Galactic Hygienes, despite their violent tendencies.

For thousands of years they'd been more or less left alone, at least once the Hygienes had started wiping out species that couldn't keep their hands off of others. But Davenport was a major source of unadium, one of the few useful metals that were rare on a galactic scale and difficult to synthesize. So population centers had been set up to facilitate the unadium exploitation; because of unadium's volatility and the ethico-judicial necessity of withdrawing massive amounts without disturbing the Thwaps' environment, it was a vastly bigger undertaking than the *Canary*'s current strip-and-grab operation.

Meanwhile, Registry Guidelines quite strongly discouraged exposing low-intelligence sentients like the Shaggy Thwaps to the kind of standard-tech societies that could only confuse their own tribal organization, and in which the only role open to them would have been slaves (slaves serving some irrational end, for example sexual or religious, since for any straightforward, utilitarian purpose a robot could serve as well as a sentient). Therefore, since most of the planet was given over to unadium exploitation, the fifty thousand or so Thwaps had been moved onto a series of reservations. Burran had been part of the team that policed the Thwaps, interacting with them on the ground, insuring that the mining population made no unauthorized incursions into the reservations, and also controlling their internal outbreaks of violence and making sure that no Thwap gained access to a Registry monitor. Burran's homeworld was even more patriarchal and hierarchical than those of the rest of the *Canary*'s crew, making him particularly suited to such work.

"It was a great place for him," finished Willa. "But when I got the chance to be a real pilot … well, that was my dream. You know?"

"And Burran did not stand in your way. The truth is I'm not surprised, regardless of what opinion Madaku may have of him."

"Not only did he not stand in my way, he was the one who showed me the call. And I'd always thought that if the time ever came to join a small ship, that he would at least mope a little. But he didn't even do that. He was just happy for me. Even if the *Canary* is starting to drive him a little nuts."

"He has a gentle heart, you would say."

"Oh, yeah. Everybody has this certain idea of him. But if you could see him when he's with me … he's different."

"How, exactly? What does he do when you're alone?"

Willa ducked her head, and blushed. With a shy little laugh, she said, "*That*, I don't think he'd want me to tell."

They ate in silence a while. Then Anya said, "Tell me, friend Willa. What is it like, in the hyperface? I am always curious, for it is one of the few places I have not been and cannot go."

Willa gave a little start. Normally that would be considered an impolite question, given what a sensitive state the hyperface was for any intuiter, and given the fact that voluminous explanatory tracts were available by the millions for anyone who felt like downloading them from the Registry. But of course, Anya was too exotic to know even that rule of etiquette.

Not that Willa minded—in truth, it was fun to be challenged to articulate the experience. She gazed into space, eyes unfocussing, trying to dredge up the words that might paint the impossible picture.

"It's a kind of a blue-gray space," she began, slowly. "For me, anyway. Even though there's no light—all I mean is, it *feels* blue-gray. A landscape of spheres and lines of connective force, stretching out to infinity, or as near infinity as makes no difference. Those spheres are gravity points, of course. You dart through them and between the lines, in your body that you can sense but can't feel or see. That body is the ship, or its astral proxy, or whatever you want to call it. You dart and ricochet through the gravity balls. All that part's fun—well, not exactly 'fun,' once you get that deep you're past the personality, or anything superficial enough to feel 'fun,' but 'fun' is the closest word I've got.... Anyway, the tricky bit is stopping near one of those gravity sources, but not so near you enter realspace in coexistence with it. And if you enter realspace away from *any* gravity sources, that probably means you're outside the galaxy, and good luck ever finding your way back. And of course they're going by too fast for you to ever really see them—you have to intuit from the patterns you're seeing where the upcoming gravity point will be, the one you're coming up on. And because you're going so much faster than light you've got to start braking before you actually reach it."

She stopped talking, and smiled at Anya. "Sorry, I know this isn't making sense!"

Anya smiled back at her. "So few things ever do," she said.

Willa nodded, and continued. Her eyes glazed again as she gazed back into that weird distance and said, "And once you go down that deep, you realize that the balls and the lines of force are familiar. 'You' don't realize it, exactly—there is no 'you' that deep in the substrata of the mind, that far below the level of the personality—by then you're way down deep in the fundamental symbol logic of the brain itself. Once you're there, it's a heck of a dance to maintain any sort of intention, much less the tight control a pilot needs, when you're down where there isn't even a 'you' that can want things. I can't begin to explain how you do it, I can never even quite remember how I managed.... And at that deep level, the mind's symbol logic's self-representation lines up with and manifests itself in the same fashion as the hyperface does the substructure of the physical universe itself. The deep structure of the physical universe is analogous to that of the human mind. And that's it: the amazing thing; the one mystery that never, ever stops being new."

At the word "mystery," a striking expression swelled Anya's face: something like a blissful hunger.

71

Seven

Willa returned to the *Canary* safe and sound; Madaku had to resist the temptation to say "I told you so" to Burran, even though he'd secretly been worried for her himself. Anya continued to spend time on the *Canary*, but less than before. She could come and go as she pleased now, using *Ironheart*'s own shuttle.

"She has an operational shuttle over there?" said Burran, during one of their crew meetings. "How come she hasn't used or mentioned it till now? Where was it before this?"

Willa asked Anya that question the next time they were alone. "In storage," replied Anya. They still spent a good bit of time alone together, chatting and visiting. It was mainly Anya who sought Willa out, and not vice-versa. But Willa enjoyed these times, too. She liked Anya. And besides, the woman was fascinating, a bottomless mystery.

"Who knows what other amazing stuff she's got, *in storage*," fretted Fehd, when he heard this answer. For while it might be an exaggeration to call the shuttle amazing, it was still remarkable enough just by virtue of having no other example of its make listed in the Registry.

Meanwhile Fehd started being more heartfelt in his morning offerings to the little altar he'd set up in his quarters to Gallyan, the ancient goddess of profit, luck, and childbirth (he didn't worry much about her third aspect). Whenever Fehd was around Anya, he dropped hints about wanting to trade for the suspended-animation coffin. His hints were too crude to be mistaken for anything else, but he didn't have the gumption to come out and get the negotiations started for real, so Anya just pretended not to understand him.

73

Except she did finally say to Fehd, as if in passing, "Willa is a most lovely young woman. And I do have need of an intuiter, at least a temporary one. I wonder if there might not be some way she could pilot me to the nearest population center? Someplace where I could have more extensive repairs done, and where I could engage a permanent intuiter."

"Um. I guess my first concern is, it sounds like that would leave *us* stranded." Willa had told them about Anya's claim to have a pure-cyber intuiter aboard, but the contradiction didn't bother him. It had never occurred to him to even wonder if such a claim could be anything but nonsense. "Besides, I don't think *Ironheart* should go on any long voyages till we figure out why the realspace engines stopped working."

Anya nodded, acknowledging that his first point was reasonable enough while ignoring the second. "We would need to make some accommodations for that, of course," she said, as if it were a problem that would work itself out when the time came.

Later that day, while Anya and Willa were hanging out elsewhere, Fehd discreetly scheduled a meeting with Burran and Madaku. He told them about Anya's request to "borrow" Willa, then said, "Obviously, we could never part from our intuiter that way, it would be too dangerous." With one eye on Burran, he added, in an exploratory way, "Of course, it isn't like we would be stranded out here, if for some reason Willa didn't return as soon as planned. We could always just send out a subspace communication for help."

"You're right," said Burran. "Obviously, we could never part from our intuiter that way."

"All right. Well, anyway, that's what I just said. But I wanted to talk to you two about finding some way that we *can* safely use Willa's intuiting abilities as a bargaining chip."

"If you're so excited by her suspended-animation coffin, why don't you just offer her money for its secrets?" asked Burran. He was joking, clearly; the idea of paying someone for information like that was absurd. It was the Registry that paid for information.

74

But Fehd snapped, "Maybe I will! All right? But that's a business decision, so please don't either one of you go around talking about it, to either Anya or Willa."

Madaku frowned. "I don't understand," he said. "If Anya were concerned about money, why would she sell the technology to you? Why not just upload the plans to the Registry, and take the pay-out herself?"

Fehd looked embarrassed. Burran, who had been making a fist ever since Fehd had blurted his order to keep Willa in the dark, started laughing. "She doesn't know she can upload it to the Registry, from any computer, and get billions of credits. Is that what you're counting on, Fehd? And you're hoping she doesn't realize that Registry guidelines forbid us from denying her use of our own subspace links to upload data. And you want to buy it from her before she figures it out."

"All right!" Fehd took his cap off and almost looked like he was going to throw it on the floor—then he just stuck it back on his head, since that was the simplest thing to do. "All right, so I'm a sleazy businessman. So what? I'm not the first, and I won't be the last."

Madaku was stunned. "How could she not know *that*?" It was one of the most basic rules: when you learn new data, upload it to the Registry. If it's really new, the Registry will give you a treat. Fehd really would be the first sleazy businessman of this particular type in the last few thousand years, if this sort of plan really worked out. "I mean, how is it possible?"

Burran leaned toward Madaku and spoke firmly and slowly, as if trying to impress something upon a child who's so far refused to listen: "She's from *someplace else*, Madaku."

"But still. If she just scrolled through the subspace feed for five minutes, wouldn't she figure it out?"

"I think she's been too busy hanging out with Willa to scroll through our subspace feed," said Burran. Less sarcastically, he added, "Anyway, I'm not so sure that would immediately pop out at her. It isn't as if the feed is full of sites called, 'Welcome to the galaxy, here are its unwritten rules.'"

Fehd cut them off: "Rather than offering to lend her Willa, I'm willing to offer her transport to the nearest population center, plus enough credits to effect repairs and hire an intuiter, in exchange for both the suspended-animation coffin, and the secrets of her alien code."

Madaku was speechless. Burran smirked and shook his head: "That's pretty dirty. That code alone is worth billions."

"I'm asking you not to mention that to Anya. And that you use your influence with Willa to persuade her not to mention it, either."

"Nah," said Burran. "I mean, for myself, probably not. Then again, I'm no angel, and I've been known to let people talk me into some pretty chitty things. But Willa? She'd never go for something like this, even if she didn't like Anya as much as she does."

"Okay. Well, that's fine. That's what we love about her, after all. But, Burran, do *we* want Anya to figure out the power she has, all of a sudden, while we're right under her nose? Do we want her to suddenly become a billionaire, capable of summoning mercenary warships to our claim, on a whim? Isn't separating her from such power the best thing to do, simply from a security point of view?"

Burran didn't meet either of their eyes; instead, he gazed at a point somewhere near the center of the table, and wore a wry, bitter smile. "You guys call me paranoid, and then you trundle out a fantasy like that," he said. "Sorry, Fehd, but I don't believe I'm going to play along with this one. Willa would never forgive me, even for suggesting she keep quiet."

Fehd started to reach for his cap, to push it back and forth, but he forced his hands back into his lap. "Okay, well, that's your choice, but just if you could not mention any of this to Anya, or Willa. All right?"

"I'll mention it to Willa. I'll let her handle warning Anya."

"No, Burran! Do not do that! As captain, I'm ordering you not to."

Burran laughed. "I don't think our contract gives you the right to give me that kind of order, Fehd captain. And if it does, fuck it. The only reason I never warned her before about you trying to scam her was that it never occurred to me how vulnerable she was. But I'm not going to go looking for her, so you've still got a window of opportunity." He got up from the table and walked to the door. Fehd glared after him.

At the door, Burran paused and turned back. "You know the real reason I'm not rushing to warn her off you? It's that I'm not worried about her. She may have some blind spots, but she's sure as hell not stupid. In fact, I bet she's savvier than any of us. I'd bet you all my credits she has a much better idea of what her resources are, than we do. So take my advice, Fehd, spare yourself some embarrassment, and drop it."

With that, he pushed the door open and left.

Fehd sat there, red-faced, fists tight in his lap. Madaku had never seen him so angry. "That *asshole!*" he spluttered.

It was true, Madaku reflected, Burran was an asshole. On the other hand, by taking a stand against cheating Anya, he'd spared Madaku the stress of having to choose one side or the other.

"What does he even actually *do?*" continued Fehd. "He doesn't actually *do* anything, he just acts all the time like he's the only competent one. The robot could probably do the same job as him, and then I'd save some money."

Madaku thought of that crappy robot in its niche on the bridge. For a second he was tempted to quip that, if Fehd was correct, then they'd all be glad Burran was there the day they finally needed the robot and it broke down and Burran was able to take over for it; but of course he didn't say that.

Fehd shot a finger Madaku's way. "Don't *you* say anything! To Anya, *or* Willa!"

Madaku shrugged his shoulders. Why should he? It sounded like, thanks to Burran, there wasn't going to be any need.

Fehd sent a message to Anya that he'd like to see her alone before she returned to *Ironheart*, if she wasn't too tired. No, said Anya, she wasn't too tired. So after she and Willa had said goodnight, Anya waited for Fehd on the observation deck.

He walked in, compulsively wringing his hat in his hands. Realizing what he was doing, he slapped it onto his head. As he made his way to the sofa under Anya's cool, aloof regard, he had to fight the urge to take the thing in his hands yet again.

He sat beside her and smiled. She did something faint with her mouth that could have been called a smile. Fehd had trouble meeting her gaze—it was a combination of the intimidation he always felt around her, the guilt he felt for trying to cheat her, and the things Burran had just said to him, about how she was smarter than he was. To escape her eyes, he looked out at XB-79853-D7-4. Its aquamarine glow reflected off the white walls of the observation deck. "Isn't it beautiful?" he said, gesturing at the planet.

"Mm," she said.

"I guess you've seen plenty of views like this, what with how long you've been around," he said, then turned to her in alarm: "Not that you look old! Subjectively, I'm sure you're not any older than I am."

"That's not the sort of remark that's likely to offend me," she reassured him.

"I only meant because of the amount of historical time you've seen. Or, uh, the breadth. Because of your suspended-animation coffin."

"Yes. And there were times, even before I got the coffin, when relativity played a part in helping me eat great swaths of time."

That gave Fehd a superstitious pause. There were legends of travelers from the very edge of prehistory, before the discovery of the hyperdrive, who had traveled in realspace vehicles near the speed of light, who had aged with incalculable slowness while their crafts had inched with somewhat less slowness across the galaxy. Legends, hell—there were plenty of examples in the historical record of such ancient craft being intercepted or arriving at their destination, to find that while only twenty, fifty, or a hundred years had passed for them, a whole new age of hyperdrive travel had blossomed everywhere else.

But as far as Fehd knew, no such interception had been made in a long, long time. And *Ironheart*, old as it was, was still a hyperdrive ship.

He got down to business. "Actually, what I wanted to talk about was your suspended-animation coffin."

Anya just kept looking at him, waiting.

Her inscrutable eyes made him nervous, but he forced himself to go on: "I'm a businessman, you know. Lately I've been into mining—it's fun, going out into the wild, opening up a new planet. But for years before that I was a trader." That was true, although in the modern galaxy one traded only in goods that had to be physically transported, not data and design. Most price negotiation had to do more with transportation fees than with the goods themselves.

Anya still didn't speak. From her expression it was impossible to tell whether she cared what he was saying, or whether she was just humoring his rambling small talk.

He said, "Anyway, I've been thinking that the design for your suspended-animation coffin is something I'd be willing to trade for."

At first it looked like she still wasn't going to respond. But then she said, "I'm very sorry, Fehd. But I prefer not to part with any of the items aboard *Ironheart*. Each one of them has a value which far outstrips its material worth. A sentimental value, if you will."

Fehd nodded with a pained grimace, as if to say he understood and was sorry to hear that, because in the end that sentimental value wouldn't matter. His heart rate increased slightly with the excitement of their roles, for he was picturing each of them as archetypes he'd absorbed from adventure vids as a boy: himself as a pre-Registry hero-adventurer-trader, and Anya as a dragon coiled jealously around her hoard of unadium and other exotic minerals. "I hear you, I hear you. The thing is, well, you're in need of passage out of here...."

"I haven't requested that."

"Well. No. But I assume you will. What you did request was that we lend you Willa, but I'm afraid we just can't do that."

"If Madaku can replace my subspace antenna, I can hail someone else for help."

"Sure, sure. Except it wouldn't be easy for us to part with any of our spares. And it's hard for me to release Madaku for such a big job right now, because of all the mining work that's still got to be done."

"I could send out a light-speed, realspace distress signal, go back to sleep, and set an alarm to awake me when help comes in a few hundred years."

Fehd gaped at her. "You don't want to do *that*!"

She shrugged mildly.

She looked serious. But Fehd decided that she just had to be bluffing, so he pressed on as if she hadn't said anything. "You'll need us to give you passage out of here."

"Perhaps. I take it you are not willing to help?"

"No, no, we're totally willing! Only, that's a valuable service. It doesn't seem fair that I should give it for free."

"It costs you something to take me aboard as a passenger?"

"Well, no, it's not that your presence would add any costs. That's not why the service is valuable, because of what it costs us. More like, it's valuable, because of how much you need it."

"Ah. And it is a service you would withhold, despite how badly you think I need it. *Because* of how badly you think I need it, I should say. You believe that threat will pressure me into giving up more."

"Hey, now! Who said anything about 'threat'?!" Without even noticing, Fehd took his cap off and began wringing it in his hands. He leaned in closer to Anya, almost imploringly, elbows on his knees. "I don't mean to make any threats. I would never make a threat! I'm not a threatening type of guy. But it doesn't seem fair for you to just come and take what you want, does it? And not give anything in return?"

"No, I suppose it is not fair that I should take what I want. Did I claim to be fair?"

"And, you know, the coffin isn't even much to ask for, in the scheme of things. People don't really even actually need suspended animation very often. I mean, most people would be a lot less scrupulous than me, and ask for that exotic code of yours." Now, why had he said that? His original intention had been to try to get both the coffin and the code from her. Now here he was, promising her he'd never ask for the code at all, merely for the sake of not having to feel so bad.

"Yes, that is true." Anya finally, mercifully looked away from him, and gazed out upon XB-79853-D7-4. She looked contemplative, and Fehd quivered with excitement at the thought that she was about to give in. Then she turned back to bore her eyes into Fehd's and said, "Or I could simply upload the schematics for the coffin into the Galactic Registry, no? The code, too, if I wished. My understanding is that this would gain me credits by the billions. Am I wrong?"

Fehd said nothing. His face burned and his throat was closing up. Tears of shame danced on the edges of his eyelids and he willed them not to spill over. So Anya had been gleaning the galaxy's new rules from the *Canary*'s subspace feeds after all.

Anya coolly studied his reaction, then looked back out at the planet. "And then there is your offer. I shall have to consider which option to take."

Fehd tried to laugh and make the whole thing a joke. He noticed his cap was in his hands, and flung it back onto his head. "Well, I guess you caught me," he said, then felt pathetic and so let his voice trail off.

They sat in silence. Fehd couldn't just get up and leave on that note, but he couldn't think of anything to say either.

Finally, it was Anya who spoke. But her words didn't make much sense: "In the stretch of time," she said, "the great danger is boredom. The only danger, I find. So one must create little challenges. Small games. One says to oneself, 'Of course I could do such-and-such a thing. But I will wait, I will restrain my own

81

power and only act if certain arbitrary things occur. Sometimes one says, 'I shall only act when the circumstances are right for me to cast myself as the villain.' Other times, for variety's sake, one changes the game. One says, 'I shall act only if and when I can play the poor victim. For it has been so very long, since I have been able to seem one.'"

Fehd frowned. "Um. Sorry? Sorry, Anya, I don't really follow...."

"No matter. Forgive me. Over the years I have grown accustomed to speaking to myself."

Anya stood, and went to the door. Fehd cleared his throat, and said after her, "Heading back to *Ironheart*, I guess?"

Anya nodded. She said, "Were I you, I would not feel too keenly the loss of that coffin. You might be surprised to find out just how very simple its design truly is."

Fehd ignored that. As she reached the door, he said, "I guess you think I've got a pretty low character, huh?" Immediately upon hearing the words leave his mouth, he hated himself even more. He was especially disgusted by his own faux-cheerful tone.

Before she left, she deigned to give him one backward glance. "No matter," she said. "I don't need you to be of good character."

Eight

Usually, when Willa wasn't with Anya, she was working with the guys on ship business, or else was alone with Burran in their quarters. But the next day Madaku found her in a quiet moment alone in one of the lounges, curled up in a blue chair sculpted into a depression in the silver bulkhead. She was reading her tablet.

Approaching her almost shyly, he said, "Willa?"

"Yes?" she said. Then she looked at him and, a second time, with more energy, she said, "Yes?"

He cleared his throat. "That code of Anya's?... I think I'm on my way to cracking it...."

Later that day, Anya called to say she'd like to invite Willa to come to *Ironheart* and spend the evening. To spare the crew of the *Canary* any trouble, she was willing to come pick her up in her own shuttle. Fehd still felt so ashamed that he gave his consent automatically.

But as they were getting dressed in their private quarters, Burran tried to dissuade Willa from going over. Actually, what he said was, "I forbid you to go over there." Willa laughed and kicked him on his naked backside. He was too solid and she too slender for that to budge him, not that she'd kicked very hard.

He grinned ruefully. "Let me rephrase: if it were possible for me to forbid you, that's what I would do."

"Well, it isn't."

"You're as bad as Fehd and Madaku. I know you like the woman. I can respect that. But you should be able to see that we can't trust her. If she wasn't here for the mining, then it's fishy that she ever wound up way the hell out at XB-79853-D7-4, of all places."

"You mean Burran," she corrected, and then threw her arms back around his neck with a grin. "I told you days ago: I'm naming the planet Burran."

"No you're not," he said, and squirmed out of her embrace. (Few people in the galaxy had ever seen Burran squirm, besides Willa.)

Willa laughed. It was an honest, hearty laugh, but there was a hint of sadness to it too. "Look at the way you wince! Why shouldn't I name the planet after you?"

"Well, anyway. Back to what you were saying...."

She shook him. She was so much smaller than he that she ought not to have been able to move him, so he must have been allowing his body to be rocked back and forth. "What's wrong with naming the planet after my lover?" she demanded.

He grinned, as if he thought she were cute. Which was probably true, but one could still sense a self-conscious anxiety behind the smile, a strong desire to change the subject. "Nothing, I guess, if you want to name it after some random thing. I guess any word will do just as good as any other. There's nothing special about me, though. Unless it's the fact that I love you, but even that isn't unusual, in case you haven't noticed how Madaku moons over you."

She shook her head back at him. The sadness in her smile was closer to the surface now. "You know one thing I do like about Anya? She's one of the only people I've ever met who doesn't think she's just like everyone else. I don't care if there are a couple trillion humans spread through the galaxy, you don't have to get embarrassed and think I'm fooling myself if I decide you're special enough to name a planet after."

Burran didn't reply at first. He only looked at her with a dreamy gaze, as if one of the things he loved about *her* was the way she could make him almost believe in goofy things that he knew were almost certainly untrue, because the mathematical odds were so astronomically against them.

Her arms around his shoulders, she let her whole weight dangle from his bulk, and he barely even noticed it. "Anyway. You're afraid she's going to kidnap me and make me be her intuiter?"

Anger bubbled up and out of Burran. "Yes, I am. She needs an intuiter. And if she runs off with you, we won't be able to follow. Not till we can get another intuiter out here, and by then it'll be too late."

"It wouldn't do any good. I wouldn't intuit for her."

"People have ways of persuading other people. You know that, you're not as naïve as you make out." He slid the backs of his fingers tenderly down her cheek. "She could do things to you, and I wouldn't be there to protect you."

Willa gazed into space, perhaps replaying some of the times she had spent with Anya. "I don't say you're wrong to be suspicious of her. She does have secrets. Or maybe it's not even that, exactly ... the truth is, she's the hardest person to read that I've ever met. Not because she's being deceptive, necessarily. She's just so different from anyone I've ever known. She has, I don't know, depths. But one thing I'm pretty sure of is that she doesn't want to hurt me."

"'Pretty' sure. Baby, listen. You're a genius, I know that. But you trust too much in your intuition. It tricks you into thinking that you should empathize with everyone. That's a good way to forget how dangerous people can really be. Why don't you leave the security decisions to me?"

"The *real* decisions, you mean." Willa's tone remained one of teasing banter, but an attentive listener would have heard an edge underneath it. "You come from a planet with a patriarchal tradition, and sometimes you don't even realize how much it's rubbed off on you, honey. You're happy to acknowledge my competence, but only as long as it's limited to one narrow specific field that doesn't impinge on yours."

"Maybe," he admitted. "You're from a patriarchal world too, though, you know."

"Yeah, but I left it. Going over to *Ironheart* is a calculated risk, hon."

"A calculated risk is when you gain something. What do you stand to gain, by going over to *Ironheart* for this slumber party? The chance to avoid hurting your new buddy's feelings?"

She draped herself over him again, and peeked up at him like a mischievous animal. "How about hacking our way into that alien code of hers?"

Burran had been buttoning his shirt. Now he stopped and looked down at her.

And then she told him about the conversation she'd had with Madaku earlier that day.

"Madaku thinks he may have cracked the code," she said. "But we can't sneak a message to *Ironheart*'s AI asking it to open up, because Anya's likely to intercept. For that, Madaku would need to perfect a transparent tendril, and the mutative function of *Ironheart*'s code is too fast and unpredictable for him to manage that yet. He's working on it, and he says he's got some promising models already running in our system. But for now it's better if someone goes over there and attaches the plug manually, and hopes the plug can persuade *Ironheart*'s AI not to ding a notification of its installation to Anya. And I'm the only one with a standing invitation."

Burran shook his head. "You sneaky little minx," he said, wonderingly. "Madaku, too."

"I don't feel very good about tricking her. But you're right, we do need to know what extra capabilities she's got hidden. On the one hand it's her own business, but on the other we don't know enough about her to safely let her keep those kinds of secrets."

Burran frowned. "I'm no expert on coding, but wouldn't programming a transparent tendril for a code with a base logic architecture that's foreign to the Registry be incredibly hard? Wouldn't you practically have to re-build the original pre-mutative code from scratch? Basically go back and read the minds of programmers whose whole species might have been extinct for ten thousand years?"

"Yup. But don't remind Madaku of how impossible it is, or he'll start remembering he can't do it."

He kept staring at her face, like he wanted to memorize it. "Every time I start thinking you're soft, you go and prove you're smarter than me."

"I'm not smarter—if I've learned how to be sneaky and careful, it's been from listening to you. And anyway, I can be soft, too."

"Be very careful around her. The AI analysis makes it look like this code originated with some unknown sentients, that we can't yet identify in the Registry. Maybe we can't identify them because they're not around anymore."

"An extinction event?" Willa frowned. "Okay. But why should that have anything to do with Anya?"

"She's a pre-Registry woman, Willa. Or at least an early-Registry one. That implies she's also pre-Hygienes."

Willa stared at him another moment; once it sunk in she laughed. "Oh, honey! You seriously think Anya might have acquired some code and then annihilated its engineers? Annihilated their whole species along with all trace of their math strategies and cognitive structures? To, what, protect herself from hackers?"

"I didn't say it's likely, but certainly she *might* have done that. Even the *Canary* could be weaponized adequately to destroy a planetary system. And the historical record has plenty of examples of stuff like that. Remember, the point of the Hygienes was to cut those kinds of destructive impulses out of the galactic gene pool. And Anya claims to date from before the Hygienes really got going. For all we know she could date from long before anyone had ever even thought of them."

It was impossible; it was too big an idea to wrap her head around. Before the Hygienes? No one had ever heard of suspended animation that could take one that far through historical time, without many many repeated hibernations; the only other way was an epic journey through the relativistic distortions of sublight, realspace travel. Merely trying to imagine the idea of encountering a revenant from those days gave Willa chills. For a moment she was lost in the awesome terror of the notion.

But soon she noticed Burran's mournful expression, and that called her back. She shook him, tugging and shoving as hard as she could. He allowed his muscular weight to be jostled back and forth. "Come on," she said. "Why the sad face?"

He softly ran the backs of his fingers down her cheek again. "Now that I know you're right to go, I can't try to stop you anymore."

Anya came, picked Willa up, and took her back to *Ironheart*. A couple of hours later Burran was in a small room with no specific purpose, just a place to use a tablet or consult the monitor. He was supposed to be triple-checking the safeguards along the exploitation chain's realspace links, making sure there weren't any undefended spots where someone could skim the top off of the ore, and, more likely, that there weren't any unpredicted cosmic phenomena that might prove damaging. Burran had already confirmed all this ad nauseam, but he needed something to distract him. Even so, when Madaku entered the room, he didn't look up.

That didn't stop Madaku from approaching him. "Listen," he said, softly, as if to make sure an imaginary third person in the room couldn't hear him. "Why did you let Willa go over to *Ironheart*?"

"Willa wanted to go. I knew you think I'm a thug, but I don't boss Willa around."

"Maybe this once you should have, if there's really no special reason to let her go."

Burran tried to keep his eyes on the module's schematics. How had he let Willa talk him into this? She was always doing that, making him believe that her idea was the best way to do things. No one else was able to persuade him like that.

"Willa said you had managed to break Anya's alien code." If Madaku didn't think Willa would be able to set up a link with

Anya's code, after all, then they'd get her back ASAP, even if it meant force-docking with that gods-damned relic.

Madaku looked guilty. Burran sucked his teeth and remained calm as he waited to see whether that guilty look was because Burran knew he'd been showing off to try to impress Burran's girlfriend, or, much worse, because he'd shown off by pretending to have cracked the code when maybe he hadn't, and had therefore sent Willa over there with a lot more confidence than was warranted.

Luckily, it seemed to be the first one. "Yes, it looks like I finally did," said Madaku. "But she would never try to go over and use it herself."

"You don't know Willa. Besides, if you didn't think she'd do anything with the knowledge, why did you share it with her?"

Burran knew the main reason was that Madaku had wanted to impress her. But he asked anyway, because he enjoyed watching the way it made Madaku sweat.

"Listen," Madaku said again. "I've come around to your point of view. There's something too suspicious about Anya for us simply to ignore it. And Fehd isn't going to be any help."

"What, are you so concerned all of a sudden because Willa's there alone?"

"Um. Yes. Exactly."

Burran let that settle. Then he said, "Yeah, okay, I respect that. But don't panic. Willa's more resourceful than you think."

"Really?"

Burran found Madaku's incredulity offensive. Both his mouth and his innards twisted as he said, "For someone who acts like he worships her, you sure don't give her much credit. Willa can out-brain the shipload of us. Hell, we're more likely to wind up needing her help, than the other way around."

There was a thrumming vibration through the floor, and through the console that both men were leaning on. Their eyes locked in alarm.

"What was that?" said Madaku. "Did something hit us?"

"No. No way. Not hard enough to do that. But why haven't the alarms—?"

Right on cue, the klaxon came on. Though neither man had ever heard a klaxon in real life before, only in drills, they could feel that this was the real thing—the alarm cranked itself up slowly, as if it had been asleep and was groaning at having to get up. All the lights went red, and the computer's voice, strangely distorted, announced, "Attack! Attack! We are under attack! Attack! Attack! We are under attack!..." and so on.

"What the hell's wrong with the computer?!" demanded Burran.

For a moment Madaku's eyes were wild with confusion. Burran was about to hail the captain, but he paused and waited because he could see that Madaku was groping toward an answer. Madaku said, "A hack! Anya's hacked us with her code!... She didn't know that I've partially decoded it and there are examples of her logic architecture in the system—the *Canary* must be using the models to fight back. If Anya's attack is doing this much damage with our system able to program antibodies, it would've knocked us out completely without the code." It was lucky she hadn't even bothered to peer through their scramblers and check, Burran supposed.

"She was going to kill us, now that she's got Willa."

Madaku hesitated, then said, "Yeah."

Burran wanted to run somewhere, do something, but this was the kind of thing one handled with computers—he dove onto the nearest console, even though Madaku was the superior cyber-jockey and likely to get results faster.

Madaku swiped readings back and forth with his fingers. Sure enough, *Ironheart* had launched an attack; the *Canary* AI was using the analysis of *Ironheart*'s code, that Madaku had stored in its memory banks, to breed counter-programs and fend it off, create work-arounds that the *Ironheart* code wouldn't recognize as foreign to itself. Until another nanosecond had gone by, that was, and the *Ironheart* code had mutated enough that the *Canary*'s work-arounds no longer passed. With all

Madaku's work on the mutative factor, the rates of evolution were almost but not quite matched on the two sides; so far the *Ironheart*'s rate was outstripping them, by an infinitesimal amount. The *Canary* would probably hold out for another four minutes. That was pretty good—it would mean their AI had fended off *Ironheart*'s code through billions of iterations. Everyone on board would still be dead, though.

Burran started to think that maybe it was a good thing Willa was on the other ship, after all. Even if she was a prisoner, at least she'd be alive.

He said, "The comm system's coming back online." A particularly effective work-around must have morphed into being somewhere in that system. Burran mashed the comm toggle. "Fehd! Hey, Fehd! You got any idea what's going on?"

Fehd's hysterical voice came through the speaker: "Oh gods, she's watching me!"

"I think he's in the observation deck," said Madaku, checking the ship's schematic and Fehd's locator blip.

"Fehd!" said Burran. "Fehd, calm down!"

"Oh my gods, she walks in vacuum!" shrieked Fehd. "She walks in vacuum!"

"Hey, there's something funny going on with the pressure in the observation deck," said Madaku, then another flashing red light caught his eye. "Shit, the inertial buffers are acting up. That'll make us vulnerable to—"

There was a massive jolt. They flew across the room and slammed into the far wall.

Nine

Despite what he'd just said, Madaku couldn't figure out what had happened at first. He'd never been inside a ship that had hit something while its buffers were noticeably weakened. The physicality of the experience was so far outside his ken that he had trouble categorizing it.

They were being shoved against the wall they'd slammed into. To Madaku it felt like the artificial gravity had gone wonky and had set "down" as the corner where the floor met the wall. "What's happening?" he shouted.

Burran was crawling back to the consoles. "Something's pushing us, I think."

Oh, yeah. Because the buffers were down, if they were accelerating anywhere then the inertia would affect them. But why would Anya be pushing them?

Willa's voice crackled through the speaker: "Anya! Stop it! Leave them alone!"

Anya's voice replied; she was more excited than the men had ever heard her, and was having trouble remembering Willa's dialect lessons. First she spilled out a great jumble of syllables, remnants of some unknown tongue. Then she reverted back to the Classical Galactic she'd spoken when they'd awoken her: "Wise, brave child! Thou hast learned so soon to pilot my shuttle!"

"Leave them alone! Get that thing off the ship!"

"But I am gone, dearest. Thou hast broken thy *Canary* free of my grapplers. Power down, Willa, lest thou do stress damage."

"Not till you call off your attack!"

"But it is finished."

That was true. The inertial buffers were regaining full strength, and the floor was the plain old floor again. Madaku got to his feet and went to the console, staggering through the unfamiliar miasmic feel of bruises. Burran was already upright and checking readings. All systems were coming back online, though the red alarm still flashed.

"Willa opened the hail to all channels, because she didn't know which would work," said Burran. "That's why we can hear those two talking."

A good guess, thought Madaku, but there was no way Burran could actually *know* that. Unless their bond was so strong that he did automatically know why she did the things she did.

"Power down, Willa," said Anya, trying to soothe her. She almost sounded nervous. "Power down, I'll not harm thee."

Then there was nothing more from Anya. "Willa's cut the comm channel," said Burran.

"Damn, that's right," said Madaku, "why wasn't I doing that?" He rushed to shut down all links between their AI and *Ironheart*'s. There could still be hidden portals; Madaku set the *Canary*'s AI to hunt them down, hoping it would be smart enough to recognize them all.

"Systems are back online—I see Willa, she's leaving the docking bay!" Burran was about to go tearing off after her, but he stopped short, doing a double-take at the console. "Shit, where's Fehd?! The observation deck's depressurized!"

"I see his life signs—he's alive—but he's not on the ship! She came and grabbed Fehd off the fucking ship! Something smashed through the observation window and took him out!"

Burran was already gone. Madaku spent a moment checking to see where the *Canary* was going—it was being pushed by an outside power, by the *Ironheart* shuttle that had rammed it, its own quiet thrusters offering no resistance. They were headed to the far side of the planet from *Ironheart*. Now he saw the shuttle detach, giving the *Canary* a further boost along its way with its own thrusters. For an instant Madaku panicked, but then he saw from Willa's life readings that she had exited the shuttle in time and was back aboard the *Canary*. She must have set the shuttle to detach remotely.

He raced out through the corridors. The unfamiliar klaxon was silent, but the lights still pulsed red. He paused long enough at one console to command all ship monitors to display his, Burran's, and Willa's relative positions. That way he could follow along as he ran, without stopping.

He did pause to see if he could tell where Burran and Willa were headed. Both their blinking dots seemed to be converging upon a single point, and after a moment he figured out it was the pilot room. He wondered if Burran had even needed to glance at the read-out, if he had just known where Willa would go.

He was about to go into the lift, when he realized with a start that would be reckless—the lifts might not be functioning properly after the attack. It was a bizarre thought, since it was almost unheard-of for anything ever to break down, but he knew it was true. So he slid down the nearby chute ladder three levels, then ran to the pilot's room.

Burran and Willa had beaten him there. Willa was activating the hyperface, and was about to affix the intuition bowl to her head. "What are you *doing*?" cried Madaku. "We can't jump into hyperspace, just like that! We have to plot out the jump!"

"We have to get out of Anya's sight," said Willa.

"But it's crazy to jump like this! It's dangerous!" Knowing himself how stupid he sounded even as he spoke, he said, "Anya said she wasn't going to harm you."

"Madaku," said Burran. "Shut up."

"I actually believe her about not wanting to kill me," said Willa. "Even though I don't know why, exactly. But you guys, I don't think she cares about."

Once she had all the apparatus set up, she shot them both a quick glance and said, "Better start praying." Madaku thought that was a joke, until he realized it wasn't.

He was about to protest again, when Burran shot him another, even more dangerous look and said, "I'm telling you,

Madaku. Shut up." So Madaku fell silent, figuring, to hell with it, maybe Willa was right.

But that was before the jump started, more suddenly than he'd ever known one to happen before. He had never realized how important to him those boring routines really were, until they were being skipped, and the lights were flashing funny, and there was a lurch that didn't seem to happen in any particular place, or rather seemed to have a billion different centers, one for each atom of his body. No jump had ever been as dramatically noticeable as this. They were going to die! Their atoms would be scattered!

A swimming sensation. His knees buckled; usually a voyage through hyperspace could pass unnoticed, if you didn't already know it was going to happen. Even with a clumsy intuiter, as long as the failsafes were on.

Gradually the quality of the light came back to normal. Madaku couldn't tell if he was still feeling that swimmy, nauseous sensation, or if this were only the aftereffect of it, and they were back in realspace.

Then he realized Willa was sobbing, and he knew they were back.

She collapsed out of her seat, awkwardly fumbling with the releases for the intution bowl, weeping wildly, not quite in control of her limbs.

Burran was at the console, already checking their location. Whatever the instruments said, he seemed not to believe them, and kept checking and re-checking. Finally he said, almost in a whisper, "She materialized us inside an asteroid."

"What?" said Madaku. One of the horror stories of ways one might die during a hyperspace jump was by reentering realspace at the same point as an asteroid that had gone unnoticed in the charts. For a surreal moment, Madaku thought Burran was informing him that they were all dead.

But that wasn't it. "A cavern inside one of these asteroids, circling XB-79853-D7-4. One of our drone probes charted it. There's just enough space to nestle the *Canary* inside. She's hidden us, but good."

Madaku only continued to gape in mystified horror. "But you mean we're still in the system? With *Ironheart*? But why? Wouldn't it have been just as easy to jump a billion miles away? Easier, even, because she wouldn't have to risk our lives squeezing into this asteroid!"

Burran smiled tightly, as if he were holding back some stronger reaction. "For Fehd, man," he said. "*Willa* knows we can't just leave him behind."

Willa was still on the floor, sobbing and spluttering, oblivious to them both. Burran knelt down and gathered her into his arms, rubbing her shaking back. "You're the best," he murmured. "You're the best."

Ten

Once Willa was calmed down and cleaned up, the three of them sat down over some tea and Willa told them what had happened. Once she'd arrived on board *Ironheart*, Anya gently told her that she was never again to leave. Anya had an errand to run over to the *Canary*. If Willa behaved, she would do her best to spare the lives of Burran and Madaku. Except for some hysterical weeping she whipped up, Willa basically went along with Anya's instructions.

After Anya left, Willa slapped a translation plug onto the nearest console and accessed the ship's computer, ordering the plug to adjust the readings and instrument controls to Modern Galactic Standard, Human. She assumed she would only have at the absolute maximum a minute to wreak havoc, before Anya saw her from her own console and ejected her from the system. But once logged in she saw that Anya had already left *Ironheart*, in a different craft than the shuttle. Since she hadn't bothered to set any locks or safeguards behind her, Willa was able to run back to the shuttle without being stopped.

"I guess she really wasn't expecting you to crack that code," said Burran to Madaku, looking at him with grudging respect.

Willa didn't understand the fine points of the shuttle's controls, but with the aid of the plug she was able to tear it out of its docking port and accelerate it back toward the *Canary*. The scanners gave her weird readings from the ship's vicinity, and she couldn't figure out exactly how to decipher them. But before long the *Canary* was visible with the naked eye, and seconds after that Anya's craft was also in view, a strange little thing floating near the hull by the observation deck, with tentacles waving in space like something alive. It was that craft which must have broken through the transparent plasteel of the observation window. Willa spent so much time trying to figure out how to shoot at the tentacled craft that she didn't have time to learn how to stop; the best she could manage was to angle the shuttle so that when it hit the airlock neither ship was damaged too badly.

"But how did that disable Anya's craft?" asked Madaku.

"I have no idea," said Willa. "The plan wasn't to ram the *Canary*, the plan was to shoot Anya's tentacle-ship. I rammed the *Canary* partly because I couldn't figure out how to stop, partly because I figured I could bore through the hull and force-dock, as long as I could instruct our AI to let me in. Then once I was inside I ran to the pilot room so I could jump us out. I was gambling that I could get us away before she boarded."

Burran was going over what little data they had from the attack. Anya's hack had mangled most of their deep data from the ten minutes before the jump, and he was mainly left with only video footage of the attack, in a variety of spectra. "I don't think you damaged her craft, babe." He squinted at his monitor, as if that would help him see it better. "It looks like she just backed off, once you force-docked." He looked up at Madaku. "And readings show that, before we jumped, *Ironheart*'s thrusters were operational. I thought her realspace engines weren't working?"

Madaku remembered how he hadn't been able to find anything wrong with them, how mysterious their malfunction had been. He remembered the strange patterns of decay they'd picked up from her scramblers. What if the *Ironheart* AI had been functioning perfectly well, and the decay had been a camouflage, a false overlay on top of the real readings? "I guess she lied about it," he said, flustered, embarrassed.

Willa's face squeezed itself together like a fist. "I'm so *mad* at Anya!"

"What did Fehd mean?" said Burran. "'She walks in vacuum'?"

"There are lots of religions and legends about creatures traveling through vacuum," said Madaku. "Lots of bogeymen.

You know how superstitious Fehd is. Something must have scared the crap out of him so bad he reverted to childhood, and then when he looked out the observation port he, I don't know, he thought he saw her floating out there with no spacesuit, maybe."

Both Willa and Burran frowned dubiously, but neither contested his theory.

"We've got to figure out some way to get Fehd back," said Burran.

"I'll go with you," said Willa.

"No you won't." Before she could argue, Burran said, "Anyway, you've got to stay with the *Canary* in case we need to hyperspace out real quick, once we get back."

Madaku didn't say anything. He was ashamed of the way his eyes kept twitching down to check the passive receiver on the room's doctor, in the hopes that Fehd would have died. But the beacon constantly broadcasting from his brain-chip confirmed his continuing survival. To find out anything more specific about his condition they would have needed to engage a link, which, unless it were couched in a transparent tendril, *Ironheart* would have been able to detect and trace back to their location, and use to hack into their system. Since Fehd was alive, they would have to rescue him. Madaku understood the necessity of that. But it would be by far the most dangerous thing he had ever done, and he couldn't help but wish for a reprieve.

They were all alone out here, though. If they tried to send a subspace distress call, Anya would detect it. No matter how fast rescuers arrived, *Ironheart* would arrive faster.

Meanwhile, they had switched off the chips in their own brains, as well as asking the *Canary*'s AI to shut off all ship's emissions—only self-contained systems were running, and as far as they could tell they were transmitting no data. Madaku had never before even considered neutralizing his brain-chip. According to the doctor, he no longer existed; he couldn't help but again and again run his eyes over the black spot where his readings used to be. And because they'd muffled all their subspace hyperlinks, no alarm was sent to the Registry, the way Madaku had always assumed would happen if his brain chip suffered trauma or seemed to wink out of existence.

"Madaku!" He realized that Burran was asking him something; from the annoyed tone of his voice, he'd apparently been repeating himself for a while. "Madaku, snap out of it!"

He shook himself. "Sorry, sorry—what were you saying?"

Burran was about to repeat himself. But his monitor beeped—he looked down at it and froze. "It's her." At first Madaku thought he meant she was here, or in the vicinity, and his insides froze. But it wasn't that: "She's sending out a message. By fucking *radio*."

He flipped a toggle and Anya's smooth voice flowed from the wall speakers, already in mid-phrase: "... and no harm shall come. I shall not lie to you, and claim that I meant no harm to your friends. My intention was to kill them, trusting that I could make up their loss to you, given time. But such is my aim no longer. Not because I care anything for your menfolk. Not even because you do, though I hate to bring you displeasure— time would heal that, I tell you. But now I see that you are so stubborn, and wild, that you will die to keep your companions free and alive. Such passion and battle-readiness speaks well of you, and I shall honor it, both for your pleasure, and to avoid that any evil may befall you. Again I say, if you will only come on board my ship, peacefully, and depart with me, I shall do no willing harm to your companions."

"Why use *radio*?" hissed Madaku, keeping his voice down as if Anya were really in the room with them and might overhear.

"Because she knows we'll detect it passively, without having to switch on something that'll give away our position," said Burran.

"Yeah, but wouldn't she assume we'd hyperjumped out of range?!"

"Like I keep saying, we have to stick around to save Fehd," growled Burran. "Anya knows that, as well as Willa and I do."

Well, apparently he was the only coward in the whole fucking galaxy, according to Burran. Madaku kept his mouth shut, resisting the urge to say that he'd only meant they might have jumped out to the far verge of the system, in which case it would have taken Anya's signal hours to reach them. But he supposed she had the time.

He tried to calculate the quickest someone could jump in from the nearest population center, if the *Canary* jumped out of *Ironheart*'s range just far enough to call for help over subspace. It would take almost a week. Madaku knew there was no way he could convince himself that was an acceptable time-frame for retrieving Fehd (although, without an intuiter, it wasn't like Anya could jump out of the system). He had to face it that they were going to need to go in there and get him, themselves.

Gods damn it. Why the hell had she taken him, in the first place?!

Anya was still talking. "Come to me, Willa. Be my companion. I promise, nothing shall ever harm you again. I will show you worlds. I will...."

"Turn it off, please," said Willa.

Burran obeyed. "It's recording," he said. "The AI can listen and tell us if there's anything we need to know."

"What was all that?" said Madaku. "Anya has a crush on Willa?"

"Who doesn't," said Burran. "No offense, hon, but I think in addition to your lovely personality she might also want an intuiter."

"Otherwise she's stuck here," said Willa.

"And she thinks we'll trade you for Fehd, and the three of us be marooned here ourselves?" said Madaku.

"Well. We can be kinda sure she won't kill me, because she needs a pilot. That's not true of Fehd, though. And you guys would only be marooned a week or two, without me. As soon as Anya isn't hovering around listening anymore, you could send a subspace distress signal."

"It's a moot fucking point, because you're not going," said Burran.

"Anyway," said Madaku, "regardless of what she promises, she'd have to destroy the *Canary* once she had you aboard.

Maybe she would try to hide the fact from you, to keep you a cooperative intuiter. But if she lets us live then, like you said, we'll send out a subspace distress call and get the Registry after her."

"Madaku," said Burran. "You've made a great start at deciphering Anya's exotic code. Ready to apply that work to a malicious code spray?"

"I think I should be able to launch a randomized attack on her systems, yes. But I'm not confident it'll do much damage. Especially since I suspect Anya's invested more time and tech in both offensive and defensive systems than are in any AI I've ever dealt with." He hoped no one would ask about the transparent tendril, because his confidence level regarding *that* project was near zero.

"Fair enough. Let's hope the spray is enough to at least momentarily confuse her defenses." Burran went to Willa and put a hand on her upper arm. "I'm gonna have to ask you to do something dangerous, babe."

"Seems like you two are the ones doing all the dangerous stuff."

"I don't know. I'm gonna need you to hyperjump out of this asteroid long enough for the shuttle to unlock from the *Canary*—if we leave from the asteroid she'll see our hiding place. You've got to pop us into some other patch of realspace here within the system, then as soon as we're away pop yourself back into the asteroid, where she can't see you. I know it'll be rough, doing two jumps in a row like that. But you'll have to recover pretty fast, because as soon as we rescue Fehd and have him in the shuttle, I'm going to send out a radio burst to signal you to hyperjump *again*, back to that rendezvous point. And once the shuttle is docked, before we've even left it, I want you to hyperjump as far away as you can manage. And after that, baby, you can sleep for a month."

Willa nodded slowly. "I can do all that."

"No she can't!" said Madaku. "Jumping into the hollow core of an asteroid was amazing enough the first time. Do you think her luck and strength are going to hold out for a second try?"

There was a hardness in Willa's voice when she answered, that Madaku had never heard there before: "I can do it," she told him.

"She can," said Burran.

They got ready. They got some weapons from the armory—Madaku had only been there once, during the tour when he'd first been hired. Burran commanded the automata in the docking bay to attach the axe-nose to the front of the shuttle. Axe-noses were meant for burrowing into minerals, but perhaps it would be just as good at burrowing through the airlock doors. Only the airlocks, though—remembering how indestructible *Ironheart*'s strange hull alloy looked, Madaku knew the axe-nose wouldn't be any good against that.

Madaku left his brain-chip neutralized, but Burran uploaded records of Willa's readings onto his. They set the shuttle to run minimal computer systems and shut almost all sensors off, to data-starve the AI. If Anya hacked in and looked at the AI's knowledge of the ship's contents, she might be fooled into thinking there was only one person aboard, and that it was Willa.

Madaku and Burran went ahead and boarded the shuttle, so that once the *Canary* jumped they could detach immediately. "What exactly is our plan?" asked Madaku.

"We'll make it up along the way to *Ironheart*," said Burran.

Madaku assumed Burran was messing with him, so he held his tongue while Burran fiddled with the controls. He was about to break down and point out that they would be on *Ironheart* in about three minutes, assuming Anya didn't just open fire on them, when Burran pointed at a section of the ship on the schematic display. He said, "We're going to ram right up against that airlock—it's closest to where Fehd's readings are coming from. Get the code spray ready, to scramble her readings and maybe slow down her defenses. As much damage and confusion as possible. Hopefully the hack we used to get in before will still work. If not, maybe our axe-nose will be strong enough to break through her airlock while leaving ours more or less intact."

"And if it's not?"

"We'll die, I guess. Assuming we do survive, we should come out pretty close to Fehd. I wish we could just use the axe-nose to eat through closer, but I don't trust anything to break that hull. We'll go to where Fehd is, and we'll take these guns with us and will use them to shoot anything or anyone that tries to block our way to Fehd, or block our way back to the shuttle. Please remember which end of the gun you shoot out of."

"All right. I do have a basic understanding of how guns work, Burran."

"We should have done all that combat practice, the way I wanted to all along."

There was a lurch somewhere deep under the floors of their stomachs, there was a sensation somewhere between nausea an an erotic tickle. It was the hyperjump. Still dizzy, Burran detached the shuttle from the *Canary*, the AI already prepared to automatically lock in on *Ironheart*. Madaku hoped that Willa was able to immediately jump back out of danger, and even more that she was able to repeat the miracle of landing the ship so precisely back inside the asteroid.

They kept the shuttle as tightly sealed against data leaks as they could manage, but listening for more radio transmissions cost them nothing in terms of visibility. There was only silence, though.

"I figured she'd be yakking away at her new best friend," said Burran. "If we were really fooling her, that is."

"I don't see any reason to assume she isn't fooled," said Madaku. "She wants Willa because she needs an intuiter. Now that Willa's on her way over, she doesn't need to be nice anymore."

"That's not the only reason she wants Willa, man."

They were coming up on *Ironheart*, bearing on the dock assigned by *Ironheart*'s AI, the same one they'd entered a week ago, when they'd first encountered the ghost ship that had proven to be occupied after all. Burran had his hands on the controls. They were going to swing around manually; programming the maneuver in beforehand would risk Anya seeing it. Madaku wondered if Burran's merely human speed would be enough.

The assigned airlock grew closer and closer through the porthole. Madaku kept forgetting that they had their outbound sensors off, so as to prevent leaving a trail for *Ironheart*'s AI to follow back to their computer; he kept glancing at the monitors as if he would see the usual detailed analyses, but they were a blank abyss.

He was tempted to ask Burran if he was sure he'd be able to maneuver around, using only his naked eye. But there was no point in distracting him. It was too late to rethink things.

"Here goes," said Burran, and hit the thruster controls. Half a second before that, Madaku launched the code spray.

Burran swung the shuttle over and around *Ironheart* so violently that the inertial buffers weren't able to entirely compensate, and Madaku felt the ghost of a lurch inside his flesh. More dizzying was the sight of *Ironheart*'s spinning hull rushing at them. Madaku had only a second in which to realize that there was no way Burran would be able at this speed to fit them into the other airlock by eyeballing it, and that they were going to smash into the hull. Then, hearing the muffled clicks of the seals, he realized he was wrong.

The airlock popped open. Madaku's code spray must have disabled *Ironheart*'s defenses, and at the same time his translated override must have outsmarted the airlock door.

But he was too scared to bask in his pride, and anyway there wasn't time. He jogged out of the shuttle behind Burran, the gun's strange bulk in his hand. Burran held his gun in one hand and in the other a tablet displaying the map schematic they'd lifted from *Ironheart*. The doctor's reading of Fehd's position was linked to the tablet. Two dots represented their position relative to the last one detected for Fehd. Presumably that was some kind of cell, because the doctor hadn't noticed him moving.

The airlock didn't even open into a bay. Madaku trailed after Burran through a dizzy, curving, narrow corridor. It was disorienting almost to the point of being terrifying—human craft generally preferred straight lines, but the interior of this ship had almost the unpredictability of something organic. At one point they found themselves running upstairs! Who ever heard of a spaceship with stairs?!

They had no need of the life-support packs on their belts. That had been expected—life-support systems were generally the best-protected, with multiple redundancies, and besides the code spray had not been designed to attack life support. What would be the point of risking their lives to rescue Fehd if they themselves asphyxiated him? Still, it was worrying that there were no flickering lights, no alarms, no odd noises, no sign whatsoever that their code spray had caused any disruption at all.

Madaku began to wonder if Anya had simply allowed them to board, for reasons of her own.

But then, as they entered a new section of the ship, he started to think that *Ironheart*'s functioning may have been impaired, after all.

At least, the lights seemed wonky. They were in the big chamber that preceded the small room in which the doctor said Fehd was being held. *This* room was a bit more like a small cargo bay, except it was too deep inside the ship. The bluish light was so dim it was hard, the first moment, to gauge how high the ceiling was.

Then again, maybe the lighting was meant to be that way, because the whole room was weird. Crates were jumbled everywhere, as elsewhere in the ship, but among those crates were other items, loose and unboxed and set in any old place. Some were little knick-knacks, what looked like glass or plastic toys scattered atop dust-caked crates, as if they'd been abandoned after an unfinished children's game, long, long ago. In the far corner, hard to make out in the murk, was what looked like the stone statue of some alien god, a formidable thing the height of two men, with three glaring eyes and a beak. And there was other stuff that seemed like plain junk, big hunks of rusted metal, primitive derelict machines whose original function had probably long been forgotten by all but the Registry and, perhaps, Anya, and which looked like they hadn't been good for much in eons.

"What is all this stuff?" whispered Madaku.

"I don't care," answered Burran, and continued toward the far door. That was where the doctor said that Fehd was.

As Burran opened the door, Madaku turned his back—the plan was that he would cover their rear while Burran loosed whatever bonds might be restraining Fehd. Behind him, Madaku heard Burran cry out. He almost couldn't bear to turn around to see why—whatever it was, if it scared Burran, he wasn't sure he wanted to see it.

He did turn, though, and rushed after Burran into the room. And immediately stopped short. "Where's Fehd?" he gasped. But even as he said it, he didn't look around for his captain. He couldn't tear his eyes from the organic thing under the transparent bowl in the middle of the room, connected to half a dozen electrodes and reflecting in its glistening surface the blinking of dozens of particolored lights.

"Where's Fehd?" he said again, his voice edging toward hysteria, his own brain refusing to recognizing the object before him. "Burran, what is that? Where's Fehd?"

"That is Fehd," he heard Anya say behind him.

Both he and Burran turned their backs on the disembodied brain, whipping around and firing their blasters at her. Madaku was so scared he started shooting almost before he could even see her.

Something was wrong. Anya was laughing—he didn't know what she was laughing at, unless it was the way the laser fire tore through her flesh, leaving smoking cauterized holes. Madaku's mind couldn't quite process it that she was still standing there, laughing and unharmed. It couldn't be that she was a hologram, her laser wounds wouldn't leave that burnt-meat smell, and anyway she didn't seem like a hologram. The psychedelic combination of the impossibility of what he saw, and its raw carnal immediacy, threatened to overwhelm him. Then Anya raised an object and pointed it at him, and something really did overwhelm him, and he was collapsing onto the floor and into blackness before he had time even to wonder what it was.

Eleven

They sat on the floor, wrists clasped in manacles attached to chains attached to the wall. Nearby were crumbling skeletons, whose bones had long since fallen out of the same kind of manacles that held Madaku and Burran, and Anya was lurking in the far corner of the room.

Really, it was wrong to say she was lurking. She was only standing over there on the other side of the chamber, her back almost but not quite turned on them. She wasn't moving; she seemed not to be doing anything at all.

Madaku slid his eyes Burran's way and managed to take some comfort from the other man's expression. None of the terror and despair Madaku felt on his own face could be seen in the security specialist's. He didn't even look very angry—he looked like a man who was making a plan. Madaku hoped he was, anyway.

He'd been planning to wait until Anya left them, to attempt some sort of conference with Burran. But he couldn't stand the tension anymore. He was about to whisper something, anything to his companion, when at last Anya began to move.

She was picking her way across the room to them.

When she began to move it was not exactly abrupt—there was no brusque jolting of one lurching back into motion. Nor was there any of the preliminary languorousness of one having to rouse herself from a daydream. Anya took her first steps as if they were the continuation of a series, as if she had been strolling a long while instead of standing stock-still for nearly half an hour.

She came to a halt and gazed down at them, her intentions unreadable. Madaku tried to control his breathing, to be as calm and stoical as Burran.

After taking them in for a moment, Anya sat on the floor in front of them, perching ramrod-straight upon her sacrum, legs folded before her and hands resting lightly on her knees. She sat out of reach of their legs, but Madaku had the impression that was mere chance, and not a precaution on her part. She didn't seem remotely frightened of them.

Madaku said nothing—he waited for Burran's cue, and Burran was waiting for Anya to speak first. She regarded them a while. Then she said, "You shall tell me stories. In return, I shall feed and water you."

Somehow, Burran managed not to look surprised by the demand. "Stories about what?"

Anya shrugged. "I care not. Any data or tales I ever need, I shall be able to download from this Registry of yours. But there is a flavor given to things by an individual consciousness. Something worth savoring for its own sake."

"And how long do you plan on this arrangement lasting?" asked Burran.

"Until you bore me."

"No. We're not interested in becoming your playthings."

Madaku couldn't help but think it was a little presumptuous of Burran to answer for both of them.

Anya didn't seem put out by the refusal. "Either you shall be interesting to me, or you shall not. It has little to do with your intention. A brave refusal to tell me tales might be more interesting than the tales themselves."

Madaku said, "And so, if we fail to amuse you, you'll just kill us?" *Or leave us to die*, he thought, involuntarily eyeing the skeletons again.

"Probably not," said Anya. "It costs me so little to keep you alive, and there is always the chance that you will do something interesting after all. Such a chance is worth the meager expense to *Ironheart*'s resources. Unless I decide it would be more interesting to kill you. But I doubt that. Killing has long since ceased to interest me much, even in its more exotic forms."

"Willa's going to be trying to kill *you*," said Burran. "You should get out of this system and away from her, now that you've got Fehd hooked up to your hyperdrive."

Madaku's head snapped Burran's way: "*What?*" he said, before he could stop himself. The notion that what was left of Fehd could be running the hyperdrive was too absurd even to have occurred to him. For one thing, Fehd was plainly dead, more or less; for another, in life he had never demonstrated anything like the level of intuition necessary to become a pilot. In fact, he'd been well below the average level for humans.

Anya gave him a weary look before returning her attention to Burran. "Your friend relies on his tools so much that he has allowed himself to become stupid," she said, nodding Madaku's way. "Men have been ever thus, since first they harnessed fire upon the end of a burning brand. But as the tools grow ever more powerful, the intellects grow ever lazier. When next I wake I expect I'll find roaming through the galaxy millions of intelligent machines, inhabited by that benign parasite of man born in their hulls who have devolved into apes and have no idea of their own origins or nature."

"Yeah, could be," said Burran, as if he couldn't care less. "Meanwhile, it doesn't take a genius to see you've got all sorts of shit here that we don't understand. I wouldn't be surprised if lots of it's never made it into the Registry."

"Yes. After long enough, the past becomes as opaque as the future. For you. And for me sometimes, as well." She turned away from them, let her eyes play among the jumbled piles of junk. "All of these items have been so important to me. That is why I brought them onto *Ironheart*. That is why I took them aboard in the first place. Yet there are so many that I myself can no longer remember. Their significance, their provenance. But no matter. They are aboard *Ironheart*. Therefore I know they are a part of me, my past. I need no further details."

She turned to the skeletons. "Them, I mostly still remember. Mostly. Though under these bones, I know there is the dust of others whose owners I recall hardly at all. Unless I am mixing memories, and attributes I ascribe to these more recent fellows belonged in fact to those of an earlier age. That could be. My memories have for so long tended to grow muddled."

Madaku tried to keep holding out, in case Burran had some strategic reasons for not asking the obvious questions; but it occurred to him that Burran might simply have zero interest in the why of any of this, only in how to stop it; besides, Madaku couldn't bear not knowing any longer. "What do you want Willa for? And what *are* you?"

Anya turned that blank gaze upon him again. But in her tone there was something almost akin to pleasure, or approval: "So. Thou hast finally realized that I am not simply a human being who began going into cryosleep a few thousand years ago?"

Neither Burran nor Madaku said anything. Madaku felt his ragged breath heaving in and out of his chest, and was sure his eyes were telling her plainly enough that he had, indeed, realized that.

She looked away from him, off into some obscure point upon the wall behind them. "Yet I know not how to tell thee what I am." Despite the distant, almost entranced quality of her voice, she didn't slump, as if her body had so long been accustomed to this posture that it required no attention from her to maintain it. She said, "It seems to me that once I did know, long ago, in what I suppose were early days. And then, I think, one day I found I'd ceased to know. I had let a thousand years pass without ever holding the knowledge clearly in my mind, and it had had time to decay, to splinter as it had become fused to the memories of other times, of dreams and suchlike. And now, so so much later, I would not dare to guess which of my nonsensical memories are rooted in truth and which are not."

Madaku stared at her. He was still trying to get his breathing under control, but it was getting harder and harder.

She continued: "My first memories that I feel sure more or less happened, cloudy though they are, are of being brought by servants into a fertile river valley cutting through a desert land. Already then I was very old—but I can remember for certain none of the things that had passed before then, although to this very day sometimes as I sleep a word will pop unbidden into my conscious mind, an inconsequential word, from one of those ancient tongues that predate the wheel, a word that has remained pure and uncorrupted in the cryostorage of my mind, that still retains its original form because I have not thought of it in so long, have not mingled it with other words and memories. Of course, as soon as I remember it, that long-delayed corrupting process begins. It comes and joins this world. Within seconds of its exposure to air it begins to fade, it loses much of that vividness it had upon its first appearance.

"As for when I came upon *Ironheart*, ask me not. Often it seems as though I have always lived upon her, even in those distant days when I rode horses upon the home planet. I know that isn't true, but I do think *Ironheart* is very old. It seems to me that I acquired her original hull, the one underneath the centuries of encrustations and additions, around the time humans were contacted by their first starfaring species. Perhaps *Ironheart* even originally belonged to those voyagers, whatever it was they were called."

Madaku looked over at Burran for some sign that he was rejecting this ridiculous story, but there was none. Madaku was no big history buff, and wasn't certain which space-faring species had been the first to make contact with humans nor how many millennia ago that had been. Long ago, anyway; long, long before the Registry, long before the Hygienes.

Anya said, "In that way-back time of my first sure memories, they brought me into that rich valley. In the land where I had been living, powerful men built temples from mud bricks, and the valley-dwellers wanted me to guide them how to build such temples. In this new place there was much large stone. But the sacred way was to build the temple with bricks, so I made them break the big stones into brick-sized pieces and build with those. Later, after I moved on, innovators chose to forego that step and build the temples directly out of massive stone. Everything changes." She came out of her reverie enough to look with distant hope at her captives. "That land was called Egypt. Have either of you heard of Egypt?"

They stared back at her blankly. The name meant nothing to either of them.

Disappointed but unsurprised, she returned her gaze to that obscure point. "For a very long time people talked about Egypt, and so I was able to remember it. It almost began to seem that it would always be remembered. But now it is long gone. And as the eons go by, and no one mentions it to me ever again, I gradually will come to forget it too.

"They worshipped me there, as I had been worshipped elsewhere before, as I have been worshipped since. They had a god-king—later they called this king a 'pharaoh,' but in the very beginning the god-king was merely called the 'husband,' because he was only the man whom I chose to marry. But I don't think I married many generations of them, before moving on. And I don't think I made any of them my companions, as I wish to do for Willa. Probably none of them pleased me, though I was more easily pleased in those days. Perhaps I had not yet learned how to make a companion. I cannot remember how I learned, or if it is a thing I always knew how to do."

"What kind of 'companionship' is it you want Willa for?" growled Burran. "You want to chain her up, like you've done us?"

"But no. You are not my companions. You are my prisoners. I shall not treat her as I do you."

"She's not going to just hang out with you, when you've got us chained up down here."

"I shall not allow her access to this dungeon—I shall tell her you have both died, so that she may stop thinking of you. If need be I will kill you both and flush you out the airlock before she comes upon you."

"You're crazy," said Madaku. "We're her friends! Her crewmates! Burran is her lover. You think she's going to want to be your companion after you harm us? She's going to hate you!"

"Ah, your error is that you see with mortal eyes. Right you are, that the hatred she will feel for me shall be more than

116

enough for a whole human lifetime: enough for two, three, four. But I can wait. And as centuries pass, centuries which none but I shall have shared with her, she will find it harder and harder to remember why she ever found anything in the paltry span of her life till now worthy of such passion.

"And as the centuries pile and stretch, she shall seep into my being, as well. A day will come when I shall look upon her and it shall seem she has always been there, by my side. At my age, one longs for sensations such as that."

Burran said, "So pick one of us instead, if you need a buddy so bad." Madaku had actually begun to wonder if the immortality Anya claimed to offer would really be so bad—it might be nice to live forever. But from the tone of Burran's voice as he offered himself, Madaku could tell he didn't think it would be so hot.

Not that he need have worried on his own account, to judge by the distaste on Anya's curled lips as she pulled her head back in physical disgust. "*You* shall not be my companion."

"Why not? If all you want is someone to get used to. What's so special about Willa?"

"Everything is special about Willa. Know thou how many times I have made a mortal my immortal companion?"

"No. How many?"

"Less than thirty. In all these eons. It is one of the only things I have not yet already done a thousand times. I'll not do it simply for anyone—I am not that bored, yet."

"Well, you're right—Willa is special," said Burran. "And you can't just have her."

"There is little thou can do about it, weak mortal. There is little Willa can do about it, either, short of hyperjumping away, never to return. But the charming creature has chosen not to abandon you, her comrades. Who knows, given more time to mature, say only a hundred years, she might be able to find a way to avoid capture by me, and rescue you both. She is, after all, very formidable, more so than you know. But youthful and inexperienced as she is, I think I need not worry on that account...."

With those last words, Anya rose smoothly to her feet and loomed over them. Madaku had already started to wonder, in a panic, what she was going to do to them; so when the ship shook with a sudden crashing boom and the lights flickered, he thought it was something Anya was doing. Even when she was knocked hard onto her hands and knees on the floor, along with the tumbling crates and shattering souvenirs, Madaku desperately yanked his legs out of reach, terrified by her proximity.

Twelve

Seconds later Willa tore into the chamber, screaming and shooting; she was unrecognizable in her pressure gear, but she was the right height and as far as they knew there was no one else in the system, so they assumed it was her. The prisoners couldn't see her enter from their vantage, but when the door opened and blaster fire darted across the room, it seemed they could hear flames crackling in the corridor.

Anya had not yet risen to her feet when Willa was upon her, screaming and blasting her till she seared. Then she turned her laser on the chains binding Burran and Madaku.

"Willa, look out!" Burran was shouting. "Don't take your eyes off her—she doesn't die!" But Willa gave no sign of comprehending. She just collapsed in between them once the chains were severed, and Burran and then Madaku grabbed the extra guns hooked onto her pressure suit. Watching her body quiver, Burran realized with a shock that she seemed to have just come out of a jump.

Anya may not have died, but being laserblasted multiple times in the face had stunned her, at least. Burran leaped to his feet and kicked her over onto her belly while the charred and half-obliterated meat of her head regenerated, then put a knee in her back and yanked something out of his belt pouch. Upon being removed from the pouch, his magno-cuffs expanded till they were big enough to slap onto Anya's wrists. They swelled into bubbles of metal that swallowed her hands.

For the first few moments Madaku could only watch, marveling not only at Burran's violence but also at his stamina. He himself wasn't sure he could even wobble to his feet.

Burran cuffed Anya's ankles as well, then marched back to where they'd found the brain. Soon he was out of view. But then Madaku could see the red flashes of laser fire, and realized that Burran was destroying Fehd's brain.

Or trying to, anyway. He came stalking back. "That fucking case it's in is indestructible," he reported grimly to Madaku and the still-hysterical Willa, as if destroying Fehd was a task they'd given him. He toed Anya in the ribs. "How do I break through that case?" he demanded. "How do I put that brain out of its misery?"

She twisted her quickly-healing face around to look up at them over her shoulder. Already her lips, tongue and teeth were sufficiently restored for her to say, "Art thou so intent on leaving me bereft of all hyperdrive?"

"I don't give a fuck about your hyperdrive. I'm not leaving my employer and shipmate like that."

There was a not-so-distant boom, and the ship rocked again. Madaku was about to point out that Burran's concerns might soon be moot, and he was embarrassed when Willa, weak though she was, managed to beat him to it. "I don't know how stable *Ironheart*'s superstructure is," she managed. "I kissed the hull when I brought the *Canary* out of hyperspace."

Madaku stared at her. At first he thought she meant she'd accidentally let the hulls kiss, and they were just lucky the slip hadn't been big enough to kill them all. But then he realized she was saying she'd done it intentionally. Any other attack on *Ironheart* might have been impossible for one person alone, ill-versed in the *Canary*'s weapons systems—*Ironheart* would have seen the *Canary* pop into realspace and its more belligerent AI might have attacked preemptively. Having the ships come into explosive contact in the first instant of the *Canary*'s existence avoided that problem. But it called for a truly unheard-of level of precision, so much so that Madaku wasn't sure he could believe her.

"If that's true," he said, "how did you manage to avoid destroying the *Canary*?"

"I brought it into realspace so that the far side of its cargo hold was touching *Ironheart*. Less than a square millimeter. I was hoping the hold would be enough to buffer the blast. And I brought it into realspace near coordinates on *Ironheart* that were removed from Fehd's position, according to the doctor—I just had to hope you were with him. And they were coordinates that were at one of the add-on compartments, since I was afraid the original hull might turn out to be *really* indestructible."

Burran wasted only a moment on an incredulous, wonderstruck headshake. As the ship buckled again, he grabbed Anya roughly by her upper arm and said, "Come on, we've gotta get out of here in case the ship blows."

"*Ironheart* shall not be vanquished!" she cried, pelting them with scorn. "Know thee how long this ship has bosomed me?!"

"Yeah, well, looks like it'll be scrap soon enough," said Burran as he dragged her along. There was a grim pleasure in his voice as he taunted her.

For the first time they saw Anya lose control of herself. She thrashed and spat in her restraints as Burran dragged her though the shuddering ship back to the umbilicus Willa had punched through the hull to connect it to the *Canary*. She cursed them in Old Galactic, and then, as her fury swelled, she lapsed into what sounded to Madaku like older, more savage languages. He flinched as she bucked and strained, giving Burran plenty of trouble as he pulled her along. Madaku more than half-expected her to suddenly burst the magno-cuffs in a feat of superhuman strength. It seemed, though, that invulnerability and immortality were the only god-like qualities she possessed.

Once they reached the umbilicus, *Ironheart* had calmed and so had Anya. The three surviving members of the *Canary*'s crew breathed heavily, gasping to regain their breath as they slumped onto the gravity cushion, letting the attractor at the *Canary* end gently pull them along the tube's length. Through the translucent, semi-frosted plastic of the thin tube walls they could vaguely make out *Ironheart*'s shape, falling behind them. Unclipping his tablet from his belt and checking its readings, Madaku said, "Looks like *Ironheart*'s self-maintenance programs have come online and managed to handle the damage. It's stable again."

Madaku was going over the damage reports on his tablet; Willa, still not completely recovered from her jump, had her face in her hands; only Burran was watching Anya, and it was he she locked eyes with as she smirked knowingly. "I told thee," she said. "*Ironheart* can stand up to anything."

Burran slammed his foot into her face. "You're not following Willa's Modern Galactic lessons," he said.

"Burran," said Willa, face out of her hands, glaring at her lover. "Don't kick people in the face when they're tied up. Not even her."

Burran shifted his weight and did look a little ashamed. He wasn't ready to apologize to Anya, though. Besides, she was simply smirking at him as before, the new blood trickling unnoticed from her lip to mix with the drying crust left over from when laser blasts had passed through her face and head.

He said, "If the *Canary* is in good enough shape, the first thing I'm gonna do when I get back aboard is smelt your ship."

Now that smirk was gone, at least. In its place she fixed on Burran a hard, murderous glare. It should have been enough to make even him nervous, though if it did he did a pretty good job of covering it up.

He said, "Gonna fucking smelt you, too."

When Anya answered, her voice seemed devoid of boastfulness. Instead, she sounded almost regretful: "Many, many are those who have tried to kill me. Sometimes I think I can dimly remember a time when a few of them caused me fear. But that is long since, and I have learned not to fear such as you."

"So maybe it's true that I could kick you forever without killing you. Which, by the way, is not an unpleasant prospect. But I bet dropping you right smack into this system's star would do the trick."

"Yes, it might, at that." Anya sounded almost cheerful at the possibility. "No one has ever done it to me. Two wakings ago the ship's crew which found me did try to do that very thing, but I foiled their plan and killed them. But my last companion killed herself that way. At least, I hope she did—I hope her suicide attempt worked—as she was piloting her stolen shuttle into the sun, I cried out to her over the comm to consider how ghastly it would be if her gamble proved wrong—if she spent the next millions of years boiling in the heat of a sun, never healing but never quite dying either. How horrible! But I think it would be enough, to dive into a star. But I shall never try. I shall live, and live, and live."

"Why did your companion want to kill herself?" asked Willa.

"She was weak, friend Willa. Not like you. You, I feel, could be the one, at long last. It takes strength to swallow the boredom. To build sinews of it. None have ever had that strength but I. How can that be, I've so often asked! Yet I suppose that making a companion is one of the few things I've not done *so* many times, since usually they last at least a thousand years, and in between each one I sometimes wait millennia. Waiting to stop grieving the last one, and then waiting to find someone interesting enough to change, and to invite in. That's how rare you are, Willa."

"It doesn't sound very pleasant, though."

"Perhaps not the ends. And, often, not the beginnings. But there are sometimes vast stretches of interest and pleasure in between those points. Vast by your reckoning, I mean to say. Come with me, Willa. Shake off these mortals. I offer you eternal life, if you wish it."

"She doesn't," said Burran, and kicked Anya in the face again. This time Willa seemed too lost in thought to protest. Burran studied her worriedly, as if it had occurred to him that it would not be so strange if she decided she did want it, after all.

But Willa, whatever she was thinking about, only regarded Anya a little sadly.

Madaku couldn't contain his curiosity. "How do you make someone immortal?" he asked.

"I put my mouth on theirs, and will it to be so," said Anya. "I no more know why it works, than I have ever understood why my hand should rise when my mind demands it."

"How did you discover you could do that?"

"I cannot remember exactly," said Anya. "It was long ago, that first time. Back in the early days of the human race. I remember her—the companions are sparse enough that they are among the only things I *can* remember well—but I do not ever remember all the events the companions and I passed through together. But I imagine I simply put my mouth on that first one, and wished she might be like me. And probably I was as surprised by the result as anyone."

The *Canary* was coming up. They all hovered a while in silence.

Anya surprised them by volunteering her next words: "That is half the point of a companion, you know. It is very hard to find someone who can be familiar, and yet also sometimes surprise one. Especially at my age.... Perhaps I myself became immortal because someone treated me thus—my own origins are murky in the distant mists. I know only that in my memory I have encountered no other immortal aside from those I have made. And none of those have been able to bear the millennia—they buckle so quickly, so quickly."

The umbilicus finished sliding them back onto the *Canary*. They dragged Anya inside and sealed the airlock behind them; they could hear mechanisms whirring softly inside the bulkhead as the umbilicus folded itself back up and retracted its two kilometers or so back into the *Canary*. This was the section of the ship which held the escape pods and auxiliary skiff's dock.

Madaku looked around. Alarm lights were still flashing, but the klaxons were off and the place looked okay. "What you did is really amazing, Willa. Anyone else would have blown both ships to smithereens."

"Yeah, well, I did rip open the cargo hold. It's pretty ugly over there—the ship's commercially useless now, it would cost less to replace than repair." She added, "Fehd would be so mad if he knew," and started to cry a little bit, but quickly got herself back under control.

She noted the way Burran was dragging Anya along the floor, and said, "Just undo the magno-cuffs from her legs, Burran, and we'll walk her to the brig."

"Hell with that," said Burran.

"Honey, I can see from the way you're moving that you're screwing your back up even more. Just undo her feet. She's not any stronger than us, physically. We'll still be able to handle her if she tries any funny stuff on the way to the brig."

"Baby," said Burran, "you are a genius. That is absolutely true. You proved that today, for the umpteenth time. No one should have the intuitive mathematical access you need for a jump like that. But you're also an idiot sometimes. I don't give a damn how helpless this person seems at this moment, I'm not unbinding her hands or her feet. Not ever."

He paused. Madaku and Willa halted along with him as he let Anya's form lay prone on the floor and leaned against the wall, bending over to support himself with his hands on his knees. There was an edge of suffering to his voice as he looked at them and ruefully said, "You're right about my back, though."

Madaku realized with surprise that he ought to offer to help, at least until they could hook Burran and his back up to a doctor—it wasn't that he was unwilling, it was only that the notion of performing such a task of physical work was so completely foreign to him.

He was about to offer to help, but Anya spoke first: "Burran is right," she said. "I am fond of thee, Willa, but that really was a stupid thing to suggest."

Anya yanked her knees in toward her chest. It was so fast that by the time the crew registered the action she was twisting to center her body weight below her shoulders and nape, and used that base to spring her legs out and smash Burran right in the knees. The magno-cuffs weren't heavy enough to slow her down, but they were hard enough to do damage when they hit him. Madaku and Willa hadn't managed to do more than drop their jaws before Anya reared back again and sailed her feet into both their faces, jerking their heads to the side and knocking them down. Now that he was down she kicked Burran in the face, as well.

Madaku curled on the floor, his face a bubbling shrill stunned alarm of pain. Physical violence was not exactly commonplace in any society he'd moved through; the worst he'd ever experienced had been childhood kerfuffles, and this one blow out-did all of those combined. Shocked, he realized that simply by striking him that way, Anya could have broken his neck and that he could have actually died before hitting the floor. *She could have broken my neck!* he screamed in silent shock. *She could have broken my neck!* He recovered enough that the external world began to seep back into his awareness, and he saw Anya hopping away from them toward the escape pod, hands and feet still bound, clanging as she went.

Madaku wasn't facing Burran, and still hadn't recovered enough to move his head, but he became aware of the wet snuffling wheeze of the man's breathing. The sound turned into an angry moan, and then the commotion of him forcing himself upright. Madaku managed to turn his head. Brenan dipped down into his field of vision, placing his hand on Willa to assure himself she was all right. Then he went staggering after Anya.

The escape pod's hatch slammed closed behind her just before Burran caught up. He slapped the hatch once with the heel of his hand and screamed in rage, then grabbed the nearest wall-mounted tablet. After fiddling with it a few seconds, he said, "*Got* you."

By now Madaku had recovered enough that he also was able to pull one of the tablets off the wall, and he hastily caught himself up on what was happening. Naturally the escape pod had assumed there was an emergency as soon as it perceived someone boarding it, and had automatically jettisoned; and, naturally, its AI had steered itself toward the nearest habitable environment, which was *Ironheart*. But the escape pod was gone now. Burran had managed to override its defenses, which were linked to the *Canary*'s AI, and vaporized it with the *Canary*'s blasters.

Madaku released a shaky sigh of relief that Anya was dead, and made a note to thank Burran. He couldn't recall the last time he'd practiced with the blaster simulator, and doubted he would have remembered in time how to take the weapons under manual control before the pod reached *Ironheart*.

Then he noticed something funny on the readouts.

"What is that?" he asked Burran. He wasn't even scared yet, so far was he from guessing the truth.

He didn't have to specify which bizarre reading he meant. It was strange enough that the tablet highlighted it. Burran stared at his screen a long moment before saying, "It's her."

"*What?*"

"It's her."

Madaku took a closer look at the readouts. "Her corpse should be particle dust."

"It's not a fucking corpse."

Now, as Madaku took yet another look at the data, it all came together. His lungs emptied of air so that he couldn't scream. He recovered himself somewhat and looked at Willa to see how she was doing. She eyed him and Burran, her gaze weary and unsurprised.

The mysterious object traveling through empty space was not an odd piece of debris but a humanoid form. It seemed the escape pod had disintegrated around her while somehow leaving her whole. More or less, anyway; but musculature and skin were whipping themselves back into place over her reconstituted, reanimated bones even as he watched. Even her hair was growing back. Madaku checked her trajectory— hopefully she would continue streaking out into infinite space, or plummet down onto uninhabitable XB-79853-D7-4. But she kept zipping along the pod's original course toward *Ironheart*. Madaku remembered that the pod was designed to eject its contents on toward its destination, in the case of such destruction. Not that it would do the escapees any good; it was

127

to provide for the contingency of goods or cargo that might have been ejected in a pod.

As he watched the body hit *Ironheart*'s hull and begin flapping its limbs for a handhold, Madaku screamed. He recoiled from the tablet as if she might reach for him through the screen.

Burran was doing something on his tablet. On his screen, Madaku saw a flare fill the space where Anya was holding on. Burran had blasted her: a direct hit, or close enough to kill her anyway.

But then he saw that she was still holding onto the hull. The camera zoomed in and he saw it was molten steel she had her hand plunged into; the view was close enough for him to see how she snarled with pain and rage. She yanked the hand out before the steel could freeze around it. Again her skin bubbled off but then regrew its smooth surface anew, almost too fast to see it happen.

Near her the laser had burned a hole clean through the hull. She'd hit one of the add-on compartments—if it had been part of the original hull the *Canary*'s lasers wouldn't have pierced it. Madaku watched her clamber to that hole across the now-buckled surface of the ship. The tablet guessed what his focus of interest was, both from the movement of his pupils and because humanoids are generally most interested in other humanoids, and zoomed in so close that Madaku clearly saw her face as she turned to snarl back at the *Canary* over her shoulder. Dumb chance made it seem she was glaring through the lens and straight out at him. Then she disappeared into the ship.

She walks in vacuum, thought Madaku.

"She's an android!" he cried. "Burran, she's an android!"

"She's not an android," said Willa. She sounded pretty level, all things considered.

"But look at what she's doing!" Madaku shoved the tablet in Willa's direction, but she ignored it. "No organic body could do that!"

"I don't have any idea how her body works, but she isn't an

android," Willa said again. "What she told about herself is the truth, as far as she remembers it. She really does come from the very dark ages. Pre-tech. Her body can't be a machine, because it comes from the days before machines existed. Anything we would recognize as a machine, at least."

Burran had come to stand over them, his forgotten broken nose dripping blood on the white plastic floor and making his voice funny. "Willa," he said. "Are you sure? There's nothing left anywhere from humanity's pre-tech, not even the planet of origin. Nothing left as far as anyone knows, anyway."

"Well, now we're the ones who know."

Burran kept staring at her. Then his vision cleared and he nodded his head once, firmly, as if he'd only needed confirmation that Willa really believed it, in order to banish all his own doubts.

He put his hand on Willa's shoulder. "For all we know Anya's prepping *Ironheart* for attack," he said. "We gotta get the intuition bowl on you."

Willa didn't say anything, only nodded and let Burran help her up. Madaku was on the verge of pointing out that there was no way Willa could be ready for yet another jump, and that she was likely to get them killed. But then he kept his mouth shut, because Burran was right—they were far more likely to die if they stuck around here, close to that demon.

Thirteen

Minutes later, they were again inside the asteroid. Willa collapsed out of the chair in hysterics, pulling the intuition bowl from her head and shoving it away. This time she was worse than Madaku had ever seen her. A trickle of blood ran from her nostril, and the smell of excrement let them know she'd lost control of her bowels.

While she was still in the throes of her fit, Madaku said to Burran, "We can't let her do any more jumping for at least ... gods, for at least a day. Otherwise it's likely to kill her."

Burran only looked at him seriously and nodded. For once they were in agreement.

Madaku was quietly hoping Anya would get *Ironheart* stabilized enough to make a hyperjump, but his tablet showed the ancient ship resting at the same point in realspace. They still dared not use an active sensor sweep, but Anya had not deigned to muffle any of *Ironheart*'s leaking data and they passively received enough of it to be able to see her position. *She* was doing sensor sweeps, fairly "loud" ones. No matter how well the *Canary* muffled its data leakage, sooner or later the *Ironheart* AI would notice that this asteroid's mass was a bit different from what it had been when first surveyed, as part of the automatic routine of entering a system.

Madaku analyzed the damage to *Canary*, to see if the hull-kissing had caused any problems that needed to be taken care of immediately. That gambit didn't seem to have endangered them; but he noticed something else.

Burran had carried Willa to his quarters with the intention of putting her to bed, but now here she was returning with him, a little unsteady but her face washed and a new outfit on. Burran took one look at how Madaku was staring at his tablet and said, "Shit. What is it?"

Madaku looked up from the tablet and let his stricken gaze meet Burran's grim one. Then he explained that the *Canary*'s systems had held up pretty well to Anya's earlier cyber-attack.

But there was a catastrophic exception that Madaku had missed, and that was in the ship's doctors.

"The med system is infected," Madaku said, stunned. "*Ironheart*'s introduced a wild mutative program right into the root of our treatment functions." The most insidious part was that other functions, like diagnostic and homing, still seemed to work perfectly—if Madaku hadn't checked, he might have thought the doctors were functioning just fine. But if they had hooked it up to someone for treatment without noticing the program corruption, there was almost no telling what the machine would have done. Except that, whatever it was, it almost certainly would have killed the patient.

If Madaku had gotten a hangnail and tried to treat it with the doctor, he would have died horribly. Like many intuiters, Willa preferred to come out of the hyperface without using the doctor to relieve any of the withdrawal's symptoms; Madaku had always found the practice eccentric, but now he was grateful for it.

There weren't really such things as rules of engagement, because people didn't really fight wars—but if there had been, tampering with another party's doctors would be the ultimate taboo. Even in adventure vids set in older, wilder times, the most heinous villains were too gallant to even consider such a thing. And the whole reason the doctors were so vulnerable to cybernetic attack was because their defenses were always low, so that they could constantly solicit data from elsewhere in an effort to find out if their aid was needed on, say, a neighboring ship like *Ironheart*.

"It'll probably take me at least a couple of hours to sort it out," said Madaku.

Burran looked grimmer still. "What's the situation with *Ironheart*?" he asked.

Madaku re-checked *Ironheart*'s position for the twentieth time, willing Anya to leave. But still she loomed out there.

"Maybe the hyperface is damaged," he suggested. "Or the drive. Or maybe she has to do some repairs on the structure before she can leave."

"She's not going anywhere," said Willa. "Not till she tries again to get me. She hasn't put in enough effort yet to feel like she can walk away."

"Willa, no offense, but why should she care?" said Madaku. "There are trillions of people in the galaxy who aren't expecting to be attacked and are totally unprepared for it. Wouldn't it make more sense for her to cut her losses, forget about us, and jump a hundred billion kilometers away to where she can swoop down on someone unsuspecting? And why does she need to swoop down on anyone, anyway? If she's got a machine that can run a hyperdrive on any human brain at all, regardless of the person's personal skill level as an intuiter? And she's already got a brain for it?"

"For one thing," said Burran, "if we get away far enough to safely send out a subspace message and stick a bulletin on the Registry, we'll have the whole galaxy on the lookout for her."

"Even more than that," said Willa, "she's fixated on me. And she can't just give up on me to go find someone else, because she doesn't want to give up on the fixation. The fixation is the point. That's what she craves, thanks to her hundreds of thousands of years adrift. An anchor, an obsession. She gets in the mood sometimes to rest on an island, in the middle of this great big infinite sea. I'm that island now."

Madaku and Burran were done second-guessing Willa's ability to intuit what was going on in the unimaginable woman's mind. Madaku said, "So, what do we do? Just stay hidden in this asteroid in the hopes she'll get bored of looking for us and finally hyperjump?" More wishful thinking, he knew.

"She won't get bored," said Willa. "Not soon enough for it

to do us any good. She learned patience a long time ago. She can keep at something till long after we're dead."

"Well, if we can't count on her going first, we'll just have to leave ourselves. Sorry, Willa, I know you deserve a long break. But I think after you've had another few hours of down-time, we should hyperjump out. Even a short wait isn't very safe, what with those sweeps she's doing." He willed her to go take that down-time now, so that he could get to work fixing the doctor. It terrified him that it wasn't functioning, that it had already gone this long without functioning. Never had he been without a doctor.

But Willa looked at him with a mixture of sympathy, weariness, and exasperation. "Madaku, we can't just leave her here."

"Willa's right," said Burran.

"What else are we supposed to do?" demanded Madaku. "She's almost killed us more than once. Soon our luck's going to run out."

"Or hers is," said Burran. "I'd say her bill is more past due than ours."

"We can't let her go," said Willa. "She's a menace—she has to be stopped, and there's no one to do it but us. That's the first thing. The second thing is, we can't leave Fehd like this."

"Right again," said Burran, mouth twisting.

Madaku felt a sickly chilled horror shudder through him. "But … I mean … is Fehd even still *alive*, really?"

"I bet that he is," said Willa. "In the sense that there's still a mind there. I think we have to assume there's still a perceiving subject that the organ is manifesting."

"But, so, how can we help him? Hope Anya kept the body and then, if we do somehow find it, hope we can transplant the brain back inside?"

"No. I don't think Fehd's anything rescue-able anymore. I think he's just got to be irrevocably insane. I think he's in a terrified hell. A nightmare of confusion. I think Anya's probably tampered with him to the point he doesn't know he's 'Fehd' anymore."

Madaku bowed his head, and took that in.

"If we're going to be the kind of people who leave a comrade in that kind of state," said Burran, "then there isn't much of a point to anything at all."

"All right," said Madaku. "But, so, we just attack the ship and hope we can destroy the bridge? Go up against those blasters she's got? We can't go head-to-head with that!"

"Correct. But you told Willa you were working on a transparent tendril hack."

"A fantasy. A hobby. A transparent tendril is *not* the same thing as the stuff I did to hack into *Ironheart* before, you guys. It's a whole different level of impossibility."

"I don't know much about coding, but I know you're smarter than you think," said Willa. "Anyway, we don't have much choice but to assume you've managed it. You've got to try to get into her system, so we can access what's left of Fehd."

Madaku's heart sank. "If I establish that kind of link, and the transparent tendril I wrap it in doesn't work, she'll be able to trace it directly back to our location."

"We'd better hope your program works well enough to be worth the risk, then," said Burran. "And that Anya's sweet enough on Willa that she won't want to blow us away till after she's been captured."

"Even then, how are we going to destroy the brain? I may be able to get a tendril into her system. But all the tendril does is hide from Anya my interference with her computers. But what helpful interference can I manage? If I start ordering the support systems to physically destroy the brain tissue, so many other systems are bound to notice and send out alerts that I won't be able to head off or muffle them all, and she'll see it. And nothing I can do to the brain's perceiving apparatus is likely to destroy the mind." Organic brains were notoriously resilient and resistant to hacker-style attacks—they could be disabled, if a hacker were given access to them through a cybernetic interface, but no one had ever manged to feed the perceiving apparatus any set of commands calibrated so as to effectively

135

order it to not simply drive itself crazy, but to damage itself so catastrophically that it lost the ability to generate experience of *any* kind.

"I'm going to ride that tendril in," said Willa. "People have been talking for thousands of years about the corollaries between the layout of hyperspace and the symbol logic of the human mind. I'm going to take advantage of that to go in and finish tearing apart what's left of him and put him out of his misery."

Madaku stared at Willa. She really was crazy. "Yes," he said, slowly. "For thousands of years people have been talking about those similarities. Hundreds of major religions have been built around them, and had the time to die out. And in all those millennia, no one has ever managed to do what you're suggesting."

"Right," said Willa. "But I think *I* can."

Madaku looked at Burran, appealing with his eyes for him to make Willa see reason. But he only shook his head, and said, "You and I have both seen plenty of proof over the last few days that Willa's the greatest intuiter anybody ever heard of. I checked the Registry, and there's no record of anyone having ever accomplished such feats of precise hyperjumping, much less within that narrow time-frame. Not ever. She's the best, the very best there's ever been. If she thinks she's got a shot at doing this, that's good enough for me."

Without even noticing it, Madaku waited for the unassuming Willa to protest that, no, she wasn't the best, and he was startled when she didn't. She merely gazed back at him, as if no one had said anything very extraordinary.

He felt himself gasping for air, as if the insanity in the room were a palpable field filling his lungs and drowning him. "Listen to me," he pleaded. "Your thought processes have been clouded by all we've been through these past few days. Okay—a lot of things have turned out to be possible that two days ago I would have called impossible. Okay. I admit that. It's amazing. But it doesn't follow that *everything's* possible. What are the odds that we just happen to come across an immortal, invulnerable creature, the closest thing to magic anybody ever heard of, while at the same time we just so happen to have aboard the greatest intuiter who ever lived, *and* a great genius of a programmer? Which is what I would have to be to slip that tendril in without the *Ironheart* AI noticing. Don't you think that's an awful big pile of coincidences?"

Burran looked unfazed. "Let's say the odds are a million-to-one against things falling out that way. Well, we could easily be the millionth ship she's done this to. Is it so crazy to think that, in all these millennia, she might finally bump into the greatest intuiter who ever lived? What happens to your coincidence then?"

Madaku had a choking feeling, like ashes were clogging his throat. "You can't just play with statistics like that," he said. "That's cheating."

Burran's voice got harder, like he was done fooling around. "Cheating or not, this is the plan," he said. "Honor and galactic safety demand it. Now, go get your tendril program prepped while Willa rests up. That tendril is the priority—not the doctor."

There was no way out of it, Madaku realized. Stunned, he began to drift away—to go prep his program, he supposed. Good thing he'd kept at it, more in the hopeless hope of impressing Willa than because he'd actually believed they would really use it.

As he went, Willa called after him. He turned to her. She stepped forward to place a light, reassuring hand upon his chest. With an odd, unreadable smile, she said, "Actually, traveling via hyperspace is the closest thing to magic anyone's ever heard of. We just don't notice anymore, because we've been doing it for so long." With that, she turned to leave the room. Burran followed her out.

Madaku watched them go. Willa's remark struck him as a strange thing to say—he wasn't sure of its relevance. Probably it was a sign of strain. All the more reason to be wary of their plan.

But it was hard to argue against Willa's and Burran's conviction that Anya had to be stopped, and impossible tasks called for impossible solutions, maybe. Once again, Madaku prepared to go work on his tendril program. This time, for the first time, he allowed himself to fully indulge in the fantasy that it might work after all.

Fourteen

Burran requested that the AI take over piloting duties and slide them out a thin crevasse in the surface of the asteroid, since there was no point having Willa exert herself needlessly with a jump. As soon as they were out, they became visible to *Ironheart*. Hopefully they were correct in their gamble that Anya would not destroy the *Canary* with Willa still aboard.

The three of them were gathered in the pilot's room. No sense in spreading out. If they were going to be blown up, they may as well do it together. Madaku wiped his clammy palms on his trousers before bringing his fingers up to once more hover over the tablet in his lap. The robot loomed in its niche. Madaku was so nervous that when he'd entered the bridge, he'd jumped at the sight of it—having never seen the thing activate, he'd ceased to notice it months ago and had forgotten it was there.

On the wall monitors they saw *Ironheart* changing course to head over to this side of XB-79853-D7-4 and intercept them. The ship seemed in no big hurry.

Burran consulted his own tablet and said, "No weapons powered up, far as I can tell. Madaku, you agree?"

Madaku scrolled through the data, taking a deeper look at the readings than Burran's expertise would allow, checking for any deceptive code shielding or clever scrambling. "Confirmed," he said. "As far as I can tell."

Madaku looked at Willa. She sat there cool and still, her breath steady, her blink rate normal. Madaku wiped some sweat off his brow before it could drip into his eyes, admiring her courage and the poker-face she presented to the weapons-bristling ship cruising their way.

Someone would have to hail somebody, soon. Madaku needed an open, active channel to piggyback the tendril onto, otherwise it would surely be detected.

Anya caved first. "Receiving a hail from *Ironheart*," said Burran.

"Put it on," said Willa in her soft, firm voice, never taking her eyes off the monitor showing their relative positions. Somewhere along the way, Willa had become the one in charge.

Anya's voice was there in the room with them: "Ah, Willa. And Burran and Madaku, hello to you, too. Which of you is captain now?"

Madaku couldn't help but shudder at her voice. The speakers rendered it flawlessly, as if she were here in the room with them. Hastily Madaku asked the AI to add a slight distortion, just to distance her. Then he got to work trying to embed the tendril.

"Fehd is still our captain, Anya," said Willa. "We'd like to rescue him, if possible." This was the ruse they'd decided on. Like Willa had said, even if Fehd's body was still in existence and revivable, there was little chance his mind would ever regain its personality functions. But pretending to believe otherwise gave them an excuse for contacting Anya, some motive other than hacking into her system.

Anya sounded bored when she replied. "Surely, my dear, you can surmise that the process Fehd has undergone has ruined his personhood, even if one may say he remains technically human. In fact, that human quality of his symbol logic is precisely why I have need of him. Which brings me to my second point: you cannot be so naïve as to think I would give up my hyperdrive capability, merely to fulfill your sentimental craving."

Meanwhile Madaku was threading the tendril to the information being beamed to *Ironheart*'s AI, the data which conveyed to Anya's speakers the auditory content leaving Willa's mouth and which would smuggle in this hidden data as well. They'd feared that Anya would insist on radio communication again, so as to avoid the risk of such contamination, but maybe she was feeling reckless.

140

Or maybe she knew that what Madaku was trying was fucking impossible. But he shoved that thought aside.

Willa answered Anya. "It didn't seem like such a wild hope. Not after all your talk about how important I am to you and how you want me to be your companion and want to fulfill my whims. And with all your exotic tech, it didn't seem too crazy to think there might be some way for you to revive Fehd. And if I did go with you, then you wouldn't need Fehd's brain anymore. I could be your pilot. If it turned out you were able to restore Fehd captain."

Through the fevered haze of his work, Madaku's attention suddenly snapped to Willa. Something in her voice had alerted him: this wasn't merely the ruse they'd talked about. Willa was feeling out the chances that Anya might have a way to restore Fehd, and, if so, was seriously offering to trade herself for him. From the silent glare Burran was fixing upon her, Madaku knew that he had just come to the same realization.

But at the end of Anya's long, dry sigh, he knew the offer would come to nothing. His shoulders sagged in relief.

"Ah, Willa," said Anya, the distortion Madaku had added crackling across her words. "True, you are a formidable pilot, perhaps the best Creation has ever seen. But, clumsy though the mechanism I have in place may be in comparison, the fact is that it allows *me* to control the ship, despite my lack of hyperdrive intuition. And none but I may pilot *Ironheart*."

"Well, technically, you aren't piloting it. Technically, Fehd's brain is."

Anya's voice hardened, as she said, "Aye, but he now is but an appendage unto *Ironheart*, and obeyeth me as doth my right hand."

Burran was flashing Madaku a look that asked plainly how long until he infiltrated *Ironheart*'s system. Madaku tried to ignore the unspoken query and concentrate on getting it done.

Willa gave no sign she noticed their tension, or felt much of her own. "Why do you need me so bad, then? If you've got piloting covered?"

"I think you must be toying with me, child; I suspect you know the answers to such questions. Be that as it may, buy time as you can. The truth is merely that I need a companion because I need a companion. And I need adversaries for much the same reason. I am grateful to your two remaining friends, you know, for having supplied that need. After I have procured you, I may decide it is enough to beat them, and that I need not kill them as well. Or perhaps I will let them go, that I might have the pleasure of knowing I could find them again someday, in whatever starfield they roam, and defeat them again."

"Have the guys been so formidable as that?"

"Oh, no, in truth. There is no shame in that. I am very old and very strong, and wise to boot. It is not so easy to get the better of me."

"Yet we did."

"*You* did, friend Willa. And only for a time."

"*We* did. Burran did, too."

Madaku poked his head up, to flash at the room a look of protest at not being included. Neither of the others noticed, and, abashed, he got back to work.

"Yes, yes," Anya begrudgingly admitted. "But I tell you I was gotten the better of because I wanted it to be thus. It is hard to explain. If you accept my gift and become as I am then perhaps someday, eons hence, you will understand how one may crave a worthy conflict so badly, that one comes to willfully dampen one's powers of perception and control."

"If you say so. You're not doing a good job of selling me on this big gift."

"Cease to mock me, Willa." The frigidity of Anya's voice made Madaku shiver. "There are other ways than killing by which one may punish." When she spoke again, Anya's voice was swollen with the dreamy soft exaltation of a mature woman who by a romantic liaison has just been made to feel youthful again: "Ah, but once I was back aboard my *Ironheart*, how grateful I was to you all! After I knew that *Ironheart* was stabilized and that she would survive. Though there were some

142

trinkets and trophies that you destroyed, and that sits ill with me.... Still, that is no great price to pay for battle! Long has it been since I have known that thrill. Not that it has been so very long since I have destroyed a ship that was shooting back at me—but that alone does not constitute a battle, for against me those vessels never had a chance. You, though, came to fight me within my very lair. Truly, I feel something so close to gratitude, I cannot think what else it might be."

"Gee, that must be why she's arming her blasters," growled Burran.

"I can hear you, Burran security," said Anya. Madaku quickly set the computer to transmit to *Ironheart* only Willa's voice, and not remarks made by himself or Burran. "Aye, it is true I am arming them. But you need not necessarily fear. I simply like to have them powered up. Many have been the times I have come to halt in some desolate patch of space and sent my blood-red lightning ripping silent through the void."

Madaku was busy with the final touches of uploading the tendril. It was as solidly implanted as he knew how to make it. Desperately he tried to make eye contact with Willa, to signal her that all was prepared. He was afraid to say anything to her, for fear Anya might hear and glean some hint. He was too superstitious to even send an encrypted message to her tablet.

Willa was oblivious, but Burran saw him trying to catch her eye. Burran himself fixed his eyes upon her, giving her a significant look. After a moment she seemed to feel his gaze and looked his way. He nodded, once.

Willa turned to her tablet and danced her fingers over it, hooking the intuition router into the tendril Madaku had inserted, all without ever looking Madaku's way. Madaku could follow her progress on his own tablet. Once the router and tendril were intertwined, Willa reached up and pulled the intuition bowl down over her head, her calm never wavering.

Fifteen

Anya toyed with the targeting controls as she and Willa spoke. She had the *Canary* fixed dead in her sights. If she chose to fire, there could be no escape for the freighter—*Ironheart*'s weapons were not the tacked-on afterthoughts one found on ships designed under the long reign of the Registry, but were survivors of a more serious time, when speed, accuracy, and power were required for survival.

"If only I could be sure my friends would be safe," Willa was saying. "Obviously I don't mind the idea of eternal life. But I couldn't bear the thought of you killing Burran and Madaku, after I took the shuttle to you."

"Shall I give you my word I'll not kill them, Willa?" Anya knew that Willa was stalling for time. Even she had proven so, so transparent, despite her early promise. Or maybe that promise had never been there at all—maybe it had only been what Anya wanted to see.

Even now, she was compartmentalizing her mind so that a part of herself was almost fooled by Willa. She chose to trust her, and so a part of her did trust, sincerely; Anya's overmind let that trusting part steer, at least for the moment. It was a practice that would be difficult to reproduce or fully comprehend, for most humans. There was nothing supernatural about it; or, if Anya's immortality really was supernatural, and not some unheard-of fluke of the natural world, nothing directly supernatural. It was simply a series of habits Anya had gradually developed, over millennia of loneliness and boredom. During long stretches when the world could no longer surprise her, she had trained her mind to occasionally surprise itself.

Willa was still talking. Anya trailed her fingertips absently across her console. She had a biter-grabber in the hold—those three in the *Canary* had likely never heard of such a thing. She could shoot it over, have it eat through the *Canary*'s hull, find and capture Willa, then have it shoot back over to *Ironheart* while Anya opened fire on the *Canary* and its remaining complement of two.

Or she could capture Willa, zip off into hyperspace, and leave the two men stranded with no pilot, wailing their distress signals into subspace till they were rescued. Then she could track them down again in fifty years, hopefully with Willa by her side, the girl's youth still intact. Perhaps Willa would have come around to her way of thinking by then, enough that they could kill the two old men together.

Anya sighed heavily. Or she could kill them all, right now. Who was she trying to fool? Willa was not so rare as Anya had forced herself to think.

Anya still did plan to take Willa, but killing all three of them gave her something to think about while the girl prattled on. In the spirit of looking for ways to make the experience more interesting, she shut down her targeting apparatus, though the blasters remained powered up. Her blasters left the *Canary* so over-matched that there was almost no sport in it. With the foolproof targeting thrown in, it would have been just ridiculous.

She played with the manual targeting controls, seeing how well she could keep the *Canary* in her sights by using only her eyes and hand, trying to think of some reply for Willa, who was bound to stop talking soon.

Then, Willa did stop talking. Abruptly, though, so much so that Anya had to check to be sure their connection hadn't been cut.

No, the line was still open. "Hello?" she said, uncertainly. Although she'd just been fantasizing about killing Willa too and having done with the whole lot, now the prospect of losing her was unbearable. She had grown so lonely, she wanted so badly for a companion to share the void with her. She recognized this feeling well, and knew it had nothing necessarily to do with Willa, in and of herself. She had felt it before, for other mortals, and likely would again. That knowledge didn't make its current hold upon her any less potent.

"Hello?" she said again, not caring for the moment that the other two mortals could hear the need in her voice.

Maybe she would even have begun to plead with Willa to speak again. Pleading would at least be something she'd not done in a while. But then she was distracted. A corner of her monitor was flashing, flagging data related to the brain hooked into the hyperdrive, data the AI couldn't decipher.

Anya leaned over and looked at the read-outs carefully. At first she couldn't understand them at all. Then she started to think that maybe she got their drift.

There was a twinge in her belly. Entranced, she used her fingers to expand and deepen that particular data stream on the monitor.

Now, this might be interesting.

A blue-gray luminescent vista viewed from a god-like vantage, in the sense that the perceiving subject experienced the surroundings as part of itself ... except that it was also racing through the vista, flashing past its gravitational hillocks and highways of force. The subject had the sense that it had been here countless times before, even that it had always been here. And yet there was also the feeling that there was something special about this landscape, something different.

That difference was linked to a purpose that the perceiving subject seemed to be carrying with it out from some lost primordial moment (that primordial moment was the moment when the subject, as Willa, had carefully framed the intention in her mind before putting on the intuition bowl, but all such details were inaccessible now). It would not be correct to call that purpose "vague," but if the subject had tried to articulate it, the whole enterprise would have fallen to shambles. This uncanny ability to maintain a precise but pre-linguistic hold on an intention was part of what made an intuiter.

"It worked!" shouted Madaku. "By the gods, it worked!" It was a good thing he'd ordered the AI not to transmit his voice to *Ironheart*, because he couldn't have restrained the triumphant cry.

He gaped in stupid stunned joy at his monitor, trying to assimilate the incredible knowledge. His tendril had worked! He had invented something! Something new, that had never been uploaded into the Registry! He grinned stupidly up at Burran and Willa, and right away his grin froze and began to slip off his face.

Willa had kept talking to Anya right up till the bowl had activated—now she had the slack, drooling expression of someone linked to a hyperface. It wasn't particularly pleasant to look at, but it wasn't unexpected. It was the grimness of Burran's face, though, that gave him pause.

The two men locked eyes. Even though Willa couldn't hear them, an almost superstitious reserve kept them from voicing their doubts in front of her, as if it might discourage her in battle.... Just because the tendril had worked, giving Willa a path into Anya's systems that *Ironheart*'s defenses wouldn't immediately see and block, there was still no guarantee at all that Willa's radical plan to enter Fehd's mind and demolish it would come off. Of more immediate concern were the odds against Burran being able to use the entry forced by the tendril to disable *Ironheart*'s weapons, before Anya or her AI noticed the attempt and blasted them into oblivion.

Madaku returned his attention to the console, sober again. If he let a bunch of celebrating interfere with his concentration, they could all end up dead. His job was to keep monitoring and fend off any of *Ironheart*'s attempts to find and dislodge the tendril. He had to keep a space clear for Burran and Willa to work in.

Already it was taking longer than they'd hoped to disable weapons. It was hard to believe Anya hadn't noticed their interference. As to why she wouldn't be target-locking on them this very instant, Madaku couldn't guess. He just hoped there was some good reason that so far escaped him.

Now the stream of obscure data was setting off a hysterically beeping alarm. *Ironheart*'s AI wasn't sure what the intrusion was, exactly, but it did think Anya ought to be upset about it.

But rage eluded Anya, and she couldn't have built up a good head of fear if she'd tried—she'd been too long accustomed to invulnerability. What she mostly felt was something that had grown almost as unfamiliar: excitement. She had thought she'd felt that when she was fighting with the mortals, as they'd captured her, but that had been only a shadow compared to this. She scrolled hastily through the data, and saw that it was true— this was a new thing, that they'd managed to do.

Not a very profound thing, maybe. Just an extremely clever string of code. But it had been thirty thousand years since anyone had managed to slip a hack this deep into her system. Bravo to them!

It was something to do with the brain—they were feeding data to it. But of what nature? Were they trying to command it to jump into hyperspace without her consent? She slapped a block between the brain and the hyperdrive, just in case. But a second look made her doubt that was the answer.

They weren't feeding any commands to its sustainment apparatus, which might have suggested they were trying to overload its surrounding electrical field and physically destroy it. Instead they were sending some kind of data directly to the brain's perceptory and symbolic apparatus. Feeding it an experience of some type.

Anya checked and double-checked the data, but could see no way it might be provoking a physical change any more dramatic than what occurred any time a brain had a new experience.

She tapped her fingernail against the console. Could they be trying to render the brain useless to her by driving it crazy? If so, she felt a little disappointed that they weren't so formidable after all, disappointed to see such ingenuity in the service of such naïveté. There were plenty of ways for an AI or human operating via a cyborg interface to render someone insane. But the process of plugging Fehd's brain into the hyperface had already driven it so crazy that one couldn't really call it "Fehd" anymore. The cognitive structures Anya needed were on such a deep level, no one had ever been subtle enough to disable them, short of initiating physical brain death. And Anya's equipment protected against that.

But she took a second look at the data. It was doing something else—she couldn't say for sure what. That irrational excitement returned. She slapped out some commands, isolating the tendril to systems it had already invaded and forbidding it from progressing any further. Now the brain was completely isolated from the rest of the ship.

What she should do now, she knew, was destroy the *Canary*, or at least batter it so badly that it would have to cease transmitting. But she couldn't control her wondering wild irrationality, her feverish curiosity to learn the answer to this new riddle. Or better to say she refused to control it. It had been so long since she'd had a genuine mystery. Not knowing about the new extent of the Registry when she'd awoken didn't count—that was simply a new variation on an old order, a gap she could easily fill. But here was something that was *working* in a new way. Shutting it down before she figured it out would be a waste.

She felt that she wanted to be physically closer to the brain as they manipulated it, as if knowledge of their schemes might leak out its folds. As she raced down the corridor, she told herself that, besides, she couldn't destroy the *Canary* yet—if whatever they were doing worked, she might wind up needing one of those brains they had aboard, as a replacement.

Those gray twilight hillocks; those shadowy suspended orbs.... The thing that may as well still be called "Willa" forced itself in close to them, staving off the panic such proximity ignited. (Down here, below the level of memory and personal identity, Willa couldn't articulate to herself that the reason she usually steered clear of these forms was that they represented bodies of massive gravity—but that now, in this case, they were the manifestations of the deep cognitive structures of Fehd's brain, and could do her no physical harm. But even if she couldn't articulate it, she somehow managed to *know* it. That was the talent of an intuiter.)

Even if these structures had no physical manifestations anywhere, they still mimicked the behavior of physical objects … simply because the human brain is wired to experience reality in terms of a physical environment. As if she were zipping through real, physical space, Willa used the "gravity" of a nearby orb to slingshot herself around and, with her amplified momentum and a silent war cry, she launched herself straight at the next orb, planning to ram it, to effect the maximum havoc possible among these structures whose nature she could not, at the moment, remember.

Madaku worked hard to maintain the self-control needed not to ask Burran how it was going. The security specialist needed all his concentration, to make sure his hack was secure before he started bossing around her weapons—if she noticed them interfering in that department before their control was finalized, she'd surely kill them.

The other question: What kind of progress was Willa making? It was impossible to gauge. They could see on their tablets that she was doing *something*, but they had no way to translate the data into anything they could comprehend. The theory was that Willa would be able to navigate Fehd's symbol logic the same way she could the hyperscape. Well and good, but Madaku had never been able to generate anything but the fuzziest mental picture of the hyperscape. Add to that the idea that she planned to somehow *interact* with the symbol logic, not passively the way one did with the hyperscape, orienting oneself around landmarks and such, but actively, so as to bring the whole deep architecture of the mind crashing down. Madaku had never even heard of any other pilot even talking about such a thing, even as a metaphor.

They had no choice but to trust in Willa's intuition.

Of course, Madaku's big hope was that Burran would take control of *Ironheart*'s weapons, deactivate them, the *Canary* would blow the ship up, and Fehd's brain would be a moot point.

And it looked like it was the moment of truth for that ploy. "Here goes," Burran said, his finger over a button. Realizing what he was about to do, Madaku had to refrain from begging him to wait a moment longer, to be extra sure he was sure.

Anya stood in what she'd long called the Brain Chamber, arms jutted out straight to support herself on the railing as she loomed over the brain in its crystal case. What had that railing originally been intended to restrict access to? It had probably been centuries since Anya had remembered exactly, the information had not been important enough to keep it fresh by accessing it regularly.

She did remember how she'd come here to this system. She had climbed down from the desolate heights of her boredom (it was a more bone-deep and savage feeling than that, but "boredom" was the closest descriptor in mortal tongues), only long enough to jettison the last brain, voluntarily crippling herself with the grand disdain of one who need never fear death or harm, who could afford to sleep in the vacuum a million years if need be, if only something would come later and awaken her to a world that had *changed*.

There had been no problem with the engines, with the hyperdrive. That foolish mortal Madaku had not been able to figure out why *Ironheart* would not run, because she *would* run.

It had never occurred to the simpleton to imagine such duplicity on Anya's part, though.

It was insanely irrational not to cut off the *Canary*'s interference immediately, not to destroy the ship completely now that she knew the danger it posed. And even if she didn't do that, it was stupid not to restrict her attention to the data stream, which would give her at least a chance of deciphering what was going on, unlike staring at this disembodied lump of flesh. But now that something interesting was happening, she felt a visceral longing to be near the event in all its sensual reality.

"Dost thou dream even stranger dreams now, pricked on by friend Willa?" The brain's lack of connection to any sense organs posed no impediment to her speaking to it—since time out of mind she'd had the habit of talking to her possessions, both animate and inanimate, as well as herself. "Hath that clever creature divined some way to send thee a message? And, what would be greater marvel still, hath she healed thee enough that thou may hear and understand? O, that I might at long last solve the riddle of how to consume a mind, consume it truly, that I might harvest fresh dreams to dream!"

Another beeping alarm interrupted her tirade. She grabbed her tablet to see what it warned of this time. It was not that she did not feel worry, or anger—in fact, she felt fury, at being thwarted and trifled with. But underneath all that, the curiosity remained, and the desire to see how this trick would resolve. The desire was no less powerful for being momentarily silent.

"Fuck!" shouted Burran, and slammed his fist into the console. Despair and rage tore at his voice.

Madaku couldn't swallow past the stone in his throat. He didn't need to ask what was wrong—he could see from the feed on his tablet that *Ironheart*'s AI had caught the tendril-branch that was infiltrating the weapons systems, as well as the one directed at Fehd's brain. Burran hadn't been able to disable the weapons before the computer noticed his interference.

Now that Anya saw them tinkering in the weapons, they were fucked. It was inconceivable that she would not blast them out of existence. Madaku expected to be dead in seconds.

Still, he entered commands as fast as he could, coming to Burran's aid and doing everything possible to gum up the works in *Ironheart*'s weapons, even if Burran couldn't take them over. He concentrated his efforts on sabotaging her shielding, despite the fact that if she were actively fighting back—which she just had to be—there would be no hope. Meanwhile Burran launched an attack from the *Canary*. It had to be useless—Anya simply had to have activated her defenses the instant she'd noticed their meddling, and *Ironheart*'s defenses could bat away any attack launched by the *Canary*. But what else could they do?

Anya stared at the code scrolling down her tablet's monitor. It really was some amazing stuff. That was a clever little mortal, that Madaku. Even if he was also a simpleton.

She had been accustomed for so long to invulnerable immortality, it took her a few precious moments to recognize the danger. Perhaps not danger to herself—then again, while it might be true that she could spin shipless through the void of space a million years without dying, that didn't mean it would be pleasant. But the danger to *Ironheart* was real. She reminded herself that *Ironheart* was not invulnerable the way she was.

Hurriedly, she issued commands to the AI.

"Firing!" said Burran. There was no reason for him to announce the fact, Madaku could see it perfectly well on his tablet. It was just Burran's training.

Madaku stared at his readouts as the *Canary*'s laser sheared off one of *Ironheart*'s four blasters. He couldn't believe it. Literally, he couldn't—he double-checked the data. Why hadn't

Anya had time to defend herself? There must have been some aspect to this confrontation that escaped him.

"Firing again," said Burran, calmly.

Anya threw back her head and howled. It was not merely rage that spurred her, but pain, the kind of nerve-searing she'd felt a few times when limbs had been shorn off and she'd had to wait for them to grow back. More than once her head had been severed, and she'd had to wait long minutes for her body to agonizingly regenerate and push itself out through the tube of her neck.

But unlike her body, her *Ironheart* could not simply grow back what was lopped off and stolen from her.

She screamed again. "Crush and kill!" she cried, as she prepared to fire on the *Canary*. There was a confusing moment as she tried to understand why her targeting systems weren't locked on. Then she remembered she'd turned them off because she'd been playing with the idea of using the *Canary* to practice her aim.

Wait. Why had her energy defense shield fallen?

Another beam of fire reached out to her from the *Canary* and sheared off a second blaster.

"Second hit," murmured Burran. The more impossible their luck got, the calmer and quieter he became. As if he didn't want the universe to notice all the rules they were breaking.

"I can't believe it," babbled Madaku. "How could she have allowed us to get so far?!" Burran didn't bother trying to answer.

At that moment Willa gasped; she shoved the intuition bowl up and away from her head and spilled out of the pilot's chair, gulping in air and hiccupping out sobs. Even that, Burran didn't allow to distract him.

"Firing," he murmured, not taking his frowning eyes off his screen.

The *Canary*'s laser sliced off a third blaster.

Anya felt as if cold air were bathing the interior of her chest cavity. Not literally—that had happened before, when some mortal had wounded her; it had hurt. But this sensation was a kind of pain, too. On the whole, a worse kind.

She recognized the feeling, though she couldn't recall any specific time she'd felt it, any incident that would have evoked it. Maybe it was only by instinct that she recognized it: defeat.

No, not defeat: not yet. *Ironheart* had one last blaster. If only she could coax it to fire, a direct hit would destroy her upstart tormentors.

Lines of transmission between her and the ship's weapons, targeting, and thruster had been scrambled. But she had always been very smart, if not always sane, and she'd had time to gain much expertise. She wrestled with the besieged systems, struggling to regain just enough control for a single shot.

Madaku tried to keep his eyes on his tablet, but couldn't stop them from straying toward Willa. Though still in tears, she seemed to be recovering more quickly than usual. Perhaps she was rising to the urgency of the situation.

"The brain," she gasped. "Destroyed."

"You're sure?" demanded Madaku.

Willa nodded, trying to stifle her sobs and regain her breath. "She can keep the blood pumping and the flesh alive as long as she likes. But that's all there is. No more neural net—just random electricity in a hunk of meat."

"Firing," said Burran.

The same moment he spoke, the ship was rocked by an explosion.

"Her last blaster's online!" shrieked Madaku.

Anya couldn't get the targeting guide back up. She'd winged her enemy by simply eyeballing them. Her long, long-dormant sense of self-preservation was starting to kick back in, and she decided to go ahead and get out; she could worry later about vengeance, if she wanted.

She went to the hyperdrive controls. Even though all that involved was swiping the screen to a different window with her fingers, it felt like she was leaping across a deep chasm to safety. Even now, under the rage and unfamiliar desperation, there was a spark of admiration for these mortals who had proven such a worthy challenge. Even if she'd had to hamstring herself, for them to be so.

Anya hit the short-cut to the random-jump sequence. She didn't care where they went, as long as it was a point in realspace unoccupied by a star or any other object.

But when she hit the command, nothing happened. It was as if the jumping apparatus were empty. As if there were nothing inside the Brain Chamber's crystal.

Anya stared at the readouts, stunned. For a moment she couldn't move, so encased was she in horror. They had killed her brain.

The *Canary's* crew didn't know yet how extensive the damage done by *Ironheart* was, but the stabilizers were definitely among the casualties. The ship was shaking like crazy—Madaku had to grip the console to stay in his chair, and Willa was rolling on the floor. Only Burran stayed still in his seat, immobile as if he'd been too massive to budge, frowning at his console. His last attempt to shear off Anya's final blaster had failed. He was preparing to try again.

Weapons were Burran's specialty. Madaku concentrated on trying to get the helm back under control. It would be pretty hard for Burran to shoot straight as long as their guns were shaking along with the rest of the ship.

Wild surges of electricity were rippling through the ship. Madaku had prioritized them lower than helm control. But now a panel in the ceiling burst off as something exploded up there, and an electrical cable came whipping out, torn in half by the explosion and spitting blinding sparks as it snapped into the room like a mad snake, its jagged end blazing and dancing dangerously close to Willa, who still couldn't walk or move well.

Madaku accessed the schematics and tried to cut the power to the cable, assuming that the robot would leap from its niche to save Willa from immediate harm. But it didn't.

By the time Madaku realized the cheap, shitty robot hadn't activated, Burran was already leaping over his console. He put himself between Willa and the cable, and was going to push her to safety when the cable's exposed, electrified end smacked him right in the face.

He jiggled there, electrocuted, until Madaku managed to cut the power. Then he crashed to the floor, his face a black and bloody burn from nose to forehead.

The *Canary* was only partially stabilized, but that would have to do. Madaku switched to weapons control. *Here goes nothing*, he thought.

Anya was taking potshots at the *Canary*. Even with the targeting systems still disabled, her shots all nearly hit home, and it was only a matter of time.

"You fought well," she muttered to its occupants, across the void. "But no matter. Take *Ironheart*'s thrusters, it is no matter. I shall go to sleep again, and a hundred thousand years hence when next I am awakened, I'll not be so gentle. Whoever they are, I shall take their brains and their goods at once, and not dally and chat and strive to make friends."

She prepared to fire again. This one, she felt sure, would be the direct hit. She could feel it.

Before she managed, a laser bolt came from the *Canary*. Even through the stabilizers she felt the rumble of an explosion: it was done, her final blaster, her final thruster, destroyed.

Before Anya had truly comprehended the disaster's

magnitude, another bolt hit *Ironheart*, this time in the body of the ship. It did not penetrate the hull, but it knocked her spinning helplessly out of orbit, with no thrusters to counteract the motion.

Another hit. Her external sensors went off-line. As the AI scrambled to bring them back up, she guessed from the rattling that she was being hit again, and then again.

Above the shock, rage, and even fear, calmly floated the question: *Is this the end?*

Willa was crying. She crawled toward Burran as he shook his blinded face back and forth and gasped, "Willa!" His mouth and jaw were relatively undamaged. His eyes had burned down to shriveled burst beans. "Willa! I need to see Willa!"

Madaku kept firing and firing into *Ironheart*, direct hit after direct hit. He wasn't going to penetrate Anya's hull, he finally realized—it must be made of amazing stuff. All he was managing to do was to push her further and further away, increasing her speed each time a laser burst against her ship.

But he was more than happy to do that. Viscerally happy. He unloaded the laser banks on her until her acceleration was enough to break out of the system's gravity.

Ironheart's hull might be invulnerable to the *Canary*'s weapons, but without a subspace antenna the ship was effectively mute, its communications able to move only at the speed of light.

Madaku's looked down at his two crewmates, shocked that Willa hadn't gotten the doctor out yet to start patching Burran up. Didn't she realize that his wounds could be dangerous, if nothing were done? Then he remembered that the doctors had been sabotaged, and the sweat pouring out of him chilled.

Willa had calmed down, now that Burran needed her. She cradled and stroked his ruined head in her lap.

"Willa," he sputtered. "I want to see you, Willa."

"Hush," she soothed. "Hush, baby."

Madaku stared at the tableau. Then he slapped the comm toggle. There was still a light-speed channel open to *Ironheart*. "Anya, you bitch!" he snarled.

Her voice crackled through the speaker, wild and mythical. "Still alive!" she crowed. "Still alive, mortal!"

"Not for long!" But any threat he might make would be empty. It would take a couple weeks of repairs till the *Canary* was ready to even navigate through realspace again, much less through hyperspace. If Anya continued on her way all that time, there would be no way for them to hyperjump and catch up with her. Willa might be the greatest intuiter ever, but not even she could make a jump to such precise coordinates without a lot of physical objects around, whose shades could help her maneuver through the hyperfield. And even once they were working again, the *Canary*'s weak realspace thrusters wouldn't be enough to make up Anya's head start, not unless they were willing to spend many months inching up on her.

Of course, they could inform the Registry of the threat she posed, and perhaps someone would hyperjump a ship with faster realspace thrusters out to pursue and destroy her.

But then again, would they? Say anyone out there half-believed them, and sent a force after Anya. Would they really blow her up? If anyone believed him at all, they would likely want to catch and study her. And Anya would get the better of her captors … given time.

Assuming they were even willing to do something so uncivilized as hold her captive.

"Still alive, still alive," she continued, then lapsed into a taunting sing-song in some long-forgotten tongue.

"Listen to me," said Madaku. He checked the star-charts to confirm the truth of what he was about to say, then continued: "We're right on the galactic rim here, and you've just fallen off its edge. There is not a single star in your flight path, nothing between here and the Aquarian galaxy. Not a planet, not a star, not a soul. Your ship will run out of air and you will fall asleep, and after that you may as well be dead because there will be *nothing* to wake you."

"I shall never die!"

"At your current sublight velocity time and space will both come to an end long before you hit another star system. And I'm erasing all record of your current course from the *Canary's* memory banks. In a few minutes there won't be any way for anyone ever to find you again, even if they were stupid enough to want to."

"You listen to *me*, puny thing." Her voice was lower, colder, harder, stranger; Madaku could better understand now those distant, primitive humans who had both worshipped and feared her. "In all the vastness of time, I shall fall into the palm of some rescuer. Many have been the times that I have gone into some desolate place where no sentient ever set foot, and rested there, only to find the sentients followed me. Or else I have returned there, to find the place changed and teeming with thriving sentients. Though you cannot conceive it, the dark between the galaxies is merely one other such desolate place. Some band of sentients shall find and awake me, and I shall fly on as before, with *Ironheart* restored. And you'll all be dead."

"You're crazy if you think people are going to start building trillions of kilometers' worth of cities in between the fucking galaxies. Space is vaster than time, Anya—at least, this time it is, as far as you're concerned. Every last star will wink out before you escape that dead coffin-ship of yours."

"*Ironheart* lives! *Ironheart* lives, and so do I! And I shall awake, and *you'll* all be dead!"

"Turn her off, Madaku!" cried Willa.

Startled, Madaku turned back to where Willa still held her dying lover's head in her lap. He'd been so wrapped up in gloating, he'd nearly forgotten them.

"Burran's going," she said. Her voice was clear and strong, though there were tears on her face. "He's going, and I don't want him to be listening to Anya right now."

Madaku felt ashamed. "Right," he said, and cut the channel.

On *Ironheart*, Anya brought her fists down on the console again.

"*You'll* all be dead," she hissed.

Madaku watched Burran's and Willa's final moments together. Now, he would have liked to say something to the guy—thanked him, or something. But he hung back, trying to be invisible.

"Shhh," said Willa, and stroked Burran's hair, lightly, careful to find unburned places where she could touch him.

"Wanna see you, Willa," he said.

"Shhh. I'm here."

"But I wanna see you."

Willa stroked his chest. She leaned over and put her lips against his ear. "I'm naming the planet Burran," she whispered.

Burran lifted his right hand and gestured with it. "Hey." It seemed like he was trying to take hold of Willa's hand, but he wasn't sure where it was. "Hey. Hey." His chest stopped moving and his head rolled over to the side.

Madaku couldn't believe it. He kept staring at Burran, waiting for him to move; surely he would start moving again, surely he wasn't dead; it wasn't possible.

Except that it was.

They had been a special couple, Madaku reflected; they had been very special. He kept his eyes down and waited for Willa to start crying again. But she didn't. Maybe she was through with crying.

Anya listened for the sounds of any more sparks, any crackles of rogue current. Usually she knew better, but right now she truly believed she didn't need the diagnostics to tell her whether or not there was something wrong with *Ironheart*. She had been with the ship so very, very long, and knew it as well

162

as she did herself. Better. In herself there were more blank and muddled spaces.

The ship was stable. Anya was sure, and the AI confirmed it. Grievously wounded, but stable.

Anya stroked its bulkhead and whispered to it not to worry. There was nothing else it need do; not for a long, long time. Only be a box to carry her through the void and keep her company.

Ironheart strained to maintain gravity and life support. It knew that in vacuum she could only function for a few minutes before she went to sleep. Anya took pity on it. She would let it rest, and she would rest, too.

She returned to the bed these latest mortals had found her in, that once long ago had been a suspended-animation coffin but that had only ever served her as a place to sleep; she strapped herself down before turning off the gravity. Then she instructed the life support to begin its slow power-down.

Would she be awoken someplace distant, many ages hence? And many ages after that, would she have forgotten this struggle with this latest batch of mortals, who had either been more formidable than most, or else had had the good fortune to find her during one of her especially careless periods?

Perhaps what he'd said had been true, that mortal (already his name was blending with those of so many others she'd known), perhaps she was doomed to rocket through the emptiness forever. But how certain he'd seemed of it! Mortals had so little respect for the infinite reach of possibility.

Anya estimated that she had something like a hundred thousand years of subjective, lived experience, not counting all the time she'd spent asleep—buried under rockslides, floating through vacuum, once chained to an anchor and dropped to the bottom of the sea (that one, she hadn't yet forgotten). In all that time, only one thing had always proven true: she did not die.

And yet she supposed that not even her own death was beyond the reach of the possible.

Cold. Thinness of air. It came—she could feel it, the sleep.

163

As the air thinned out, she worked harder to draw it in. Who knew? Perhaps this would be her last.

She drew her hands up to rub them against her arms, as the heat leaked from the ship. Soon the temperature plummeted far below what any normal human could have survived. Instead of taking her hands off her arms, Anya drew them up higher. Until her forearms were crossed over her chest, each hand's fingers brushing the edge of the other side of her collarbone.

Her breath grew smaller and smaller as the oxygen got used up, her chest moving in tiny hitches that would be almost imperceptible to an observer and soon wouldn't be there at all.

As the motion of her chest grew slighter and slighter, she smiled. Then her smile widened, the corners of her mouth stretching back, exposing her teeth.

Yes, perhaps these would be her last few breaths. And yet she knew they wouldn't be.

Soon, she went to sleep. Her eyes were open.

For new releases from J. Boyett, and occasional free stuff, sign up for the mailing list at www.jboyett.net

And please consider leaving a review for this book on Amazon, Goodreads, or any other online forum.

Thanks again!

ALSO FROM SALTIMBANQUE BOOKS:

THE UNKILLABLES,
by J. Boyett
Gash-Eye already thought life was hard, as the Neanderthal slave to a band of Cro-Magnons. Then zombies attacked, wiping out nearly everyone she knows and separating her from the Jaw, her half-breed son. Now she fights to keep the last remnants of her former captors alive. Meanwhile, the Jaw and his father try to survive as they maneuver the zombie-infested landscape alongside time-travelers from thirty thousand years in the future.... Destined to become a classic in the literature of Zombies vs. Cavemen.

COLD PLATE SPECIAL,
by Rob Widdicombe
Jarvis Henders has finally hit the beige bottom of his beige life, his law-school dreams in shambles, and every bar singing to him to end his latest streak of sobriety. Instead of falling back off the wagon, he decides to go take his life back from the child molester who stole it. But his journey through the looking glass turns into an adventure where he's too busy trying to guess what will come at him next, to dwell on the ghosts of his past.

STEWART AND JEAN,
by J. Boyett
A blind date between Stewart and Jean explodes into a confrontation from the past when Jean realizes that theirs is not a random meeting at all, but that Stewart is the brother of the man who once tried to rape her. Or is she the woman who murdered his brother? And will anyone ever know?

THE LITTLE MERMAID: A HORROR STORY,
by J. Boyett

Brenna has an idyllic life with her heroic, dashing, life-guard boyfriend Mark. She knows it's only natural that other girls should have crushes on the guy. But there's something different about the young girl he's rescued, who seemed to appear in the sea out of nowhere—a young girl with strange powers, and who will stop at nothing to have Mark for herself.

I'M YOUR MAN,
by F. Sykes

It's New York in the 1990's, and every week for years Fred has cruised Port Authority for hustlers, living a double life, dreaming of the one perfect boy that he can really love. When he meets Adam, he wonders if he's found that perfect boy after all ... and even though Adam proves to be very imperfect, and very real, Fred's dream is strengthened to the point that he finds it difficult to awake.

BENJAMIN GOLDEN DEVILHORNS,
by Doug Shields

A collection of stories set in a bizarre, almost believable universe: the lord of cockroaches breathes the same air as a genius teenage girl with a thing for criminals, a ruthless meat tycoon who hasn't figured out that secret gay affairs are best conducted out of town, and a telepathic bowling ball. Yes, the bowling ball breathes.

RICKY,
by J. Boyett

Ricky's hoping to begin a new life upon his release from prison; but on his second day out, someone murders his sister. Determined to find her killer, but with no idea how to go about it, Ricky follows a dangerous path, led by clues that may only be in his mind.

BROTHEL,

by J. Boyett

What to do for kicks if you live in a sleepy college town, and all you need to pass your courses is basic literacy? Well, you could keep up with all the popular TV shows. Or see how much alcohol you can drink without dying. Or spice things up with the occasional hump behind the bushes. And if that's not enough you could start a business....

THE VICTIM *(AND OTHER SHORT PLAYS)*,

by J. Boyett

In The Victim, April wants Grace to help her prosecute the guys who raped them years before. The only problem is, Grace doesn't remember things that way.... Also included:

A young man picks up a strange woman in a bar, only to realize she's no stranger after all;

An uptight socialite learns some outrageous truths about her family;

A sister stumbles upon her brother's bizarre sexual rite;

A first date ends in grotesque revelations;

A love potion proves all too effective;

A lesbian wedding is complicated when it turns out one bride's brother used to date the other bride.

ABOUT THE AUTHOR

J. Boyett can be reached at jboyettjboyett@gmail.com, unless you are reading this many years after we went to print and no one uses Gmail anymore, and/or unless J. Boyett has died.

www.ingramcontent.com/pod-product-compliance
Lightning Source LLC
Chambersburg PA
CBHW060745180626
46818CB00002B/461